I0706344

Cozy Up
to Death

a novel about a bookstore,
a cat, knitting, and blood

by Colin Conway

Dedicated to Gertrude Von Finklestein

*I don't mind dying.
I just don't want to be there when it happens.*

Spike Milligan

Chapter 1

The brass bell tinkled brightly when the door to the bookstore swung open.

The ocean's aroma and the summer's humidity entered along with the older woman. She took her time closing the door, then turned to wipe her feet several times on the well-worn mat, which once read *All Good Stories Begin Here*. Unfortunately, most of the *Good* and all the *Begin* had rubbed off over the years, so the remaining message was *All Stories Here*.

When she finished cleaning the soles of her shoes, she lifted her head, her eyes widening in anticipation. It was apparent the slight woman enjoyed bookstores, and it appeared to be her first time at The Red Herring, Pleasant Valley's only mystery bookshop.

Before moving, her eyes scanned every inch of the store, passing over the huge man standing behind the counter.

When the woman felt she had a good understanding of the layout, she stepped inward but stopped suddenly when an orange cat appeared out of nowhere to rub itself against her leg.

"Hello, sweetie," the woman said, bending over to pet the scruffy tom.

It, however, had no intentions of being touched and hurried away, deeper into the store.

The woman righted herself and beamed. She appeared to be a cat person as she was not offended by the feline's snub of her interest.

"Where to start?" she mumbled and stepped toward a small display with the headline banner *Local Author Carrie Fenton*. Underneath were several True Crime books that blatantly worked Maine into the title—*The Death of Maine, Maine's Bluest Blood*, and *Maine Line Murder*. The woman dismissively shook her head and moved toward a nearby book spinner.

In the back of the shop, something fell to the floor.

"Cat!" the man hollered from behind the sales counter. "Knock it off!" His deep baritone voice was gravelly and seemed to shake the small store.

The woman stopped then to take him in fully. As she stared, her hand slowly lifted to her chest.

"I apologize," the man said, his voice returning to a reasonable level. "The cat, he knocks things over. Aren't they supposed to be graceful?"

The woman dropped her hand and stepped forward. She looked up at the man with awe. It was the reaction he got most when in polite company. He stood six-foot-four inches and weighed roughly two-hundred twenty-five pounds.

"You sure are a big fella," she said with a southern accent. "My son played for the

University of Alabama, and you're even bigger than him. Didja play ball in school?"

"No, ma'am."

"How come?" she asked as if not playing football was an odd choice for a man of his size.

He thought for a moment, then said with a conspiratorial half-grin, "It was too dangerous."

She patted the counter in a knowing gesture and gave him a kind smile. "Oh, of course. I always worried about my boy getting hurt, but my husband insisted our son play. Your father was smart for not letting you. It's a risky game, for sure. Owning a bookstore is much smarter. I'm assuming you're the owner, that is?"

"I guess I am."

She stuck out her hand. "I'm Helen."

"Brody."

"It's nice to meet you," she said. Her words trailed off as she noticed the tattoo on the back of his right hand. The ink seemed to disappear underneath the plaid, long-sleeved shirt he wore buttoned up to his neck.

Brody pulled his hand back and shoved it into his pants pocket.

Helen regained her smile and said, "Everyone in this town is so nice. My sister and I are touring through the northeast and spent last night here. I'm so delighted by the hospitality everyone has shown."

She watched him expectantly, hoping Brody would engage in conversation. Instead, he remained silent and studied her. They stared at each other for a few moments until Helen spoke again.

"We're leaving this afternoon and going up to York Harbor."

Brody's brow furrowed.

"York Harbor," the woman repeated. "It's ten minutes up the way." Helen pointed absently toward the north.

"Ah."

"But we'll be in Pleasant Valley until lunchtime. What do you recommend we do?"

"No idea," Brody said.

"Really?"

He shrugged.

"How long have you lived in this town?"

"A day."

"One day? But you own this store."

Brody hesitated before saying, "I bought it online."

"Online?"

"Through the Internet."

"The Internet?" Helen repeated before whistling softly. "You bought a business on the Internet. Who would have thought such a thing possible?"

Something again fell in the back of the store, and Brody turned his head to yell, "Cat!"

"Is today your first day?"

"I wouldn't lie about that."

"And that's your kitty?"

"He came with the store." Brody leaned in. "And if you want him, you can have him. Free."

"Oh, honey," Helen said, "I can't take him. Besides, every bookstore needs a cat."

"Not this one," Brody muttered with a look of exasperation.

Helen's face widened with excitement. "Am I, possibly, your first customer?"

"I believe so."

The woman tapped the counter with excitement. "In that case, let me buy something! I like a good mystery. Agatha Christie is my favorite, but I've read all her books. So nothing by her, okay? I also like Sue Grafton and Janet Evanovich, but I've been through all their books, too. What new writer do you suggest I try?"

A frown creased Brody's face, and he crossed his thick arms.

"If you don't know anyone comparable to those writers, you can suggest anyone, my dear. Who do you like? I'll buy any book you suggest so I can be your first customer. What a neat honor that would be."

"I'm not sure who to recommend," he admitted.

"I've stumped you?" She turned to survey the bookstore. "How is that possible with all these delightful treasures?"

"To be honest," Brody said, "I don't read."

Helen stared at him, dumbfounded.

"I mean, I read," Brody corrected himself. "Newspapers and repair manuals and such. But I haven't read an actual book since high school."

The older woman picked up a paperback copy of John D. MacDonald's *The Deep Blue Good-by* that was lying on the counter, turning it in her hand. "But this is a ..."

"A bookstore. I know."

"I don't understand," she said.

"That makes two of us."

"What?" she asked, clearly confused.

A large clunk occurred in the rear of the store, which was then followed by several smaller noises.

"Cat!" Brody yelled. He turned to the befuddled Helen and said, "I'll be back."

In the section identified as *Thrillers*, the orange cat was nowhere to be found, but several books were lying in the aisleway. Brody quickly scooped them up and stacked them on a shelf without consideration as to where they belonged. While he did that, the bell chimed again at the front of the store.

Brody stole a final glance for the cat and returned to the counter. No one was there now since the older woman had left without buying a book.

He smelled the ocean's air from when she opened the door. The summer's humidity had snuck in again, and the building's swamp cooler had yet to beat it back. It wasn't even noon, and he'd already had and lost his first customer.

Brody realized living in Pleasant Valley was going to take some getting used to.

Chapter 2

He walked to the rear entrance of the store and examined the alley that ran behind the building. Brody was checking on his truck, a 1985 Ford F-150, when the brass bell rang again. He sighed, understanding then that customers coming into the store might be a regular occurrence.

Before closing the door, he took another look at the alley. It was spotless. Strangely so. He glanced in both directions, familiarizing himself with its layout. If he ever needed to make a hasty exit from the store, it would be an accessible route. On the opposite side of the alley were a row of houses he couldn't see due to the large hedges that most of them had. If he couldn't see the neighbors, he thought, then they couldn't see him.

It wasn't a bad location, he considered, although he would soon need to walk around the block to determine who actually lived in those houses.

He pulled the door closed, locked it, and headed toward the front of the shop. He passed the entrance to the basement stairway. It was dark and empty down there—too damp to store any books—but perfect for a few old pieces of furniture.

A woman stood at the book spinner, turning it slowly as her eyes scanned each title. She wore a light-yellow summer dress that hung from petite shoulders. Her straight mousy brown hair fell into her face as she bent her head to read the lower book titles. When her large round glasses slid down her nose, she pushed them up into place with a single finger.

She slowly squatted so she could better see the books. She pulled a book from the spinner, turned it over, and read the back cover.

Not wanting to disturb her, Brody strolled behind the counter where he sat on the cushioned stool. He put an elbow on the worktop, rested his chin in his hand, and watched her.

As she returned the book to the spinner, the orange cat appeared. It rubbed itself against her leg, and when she bent over, it allowed her to pet it.

"Hello, Rhodenbarr," the woman said, her voice light and airy.

"Rhodenbarr?" Brody asked.

The woman started at the sound of his voice. "Oh! I didn't see you there."

"Is that the cat's name? Rhodenbarr?"

"It is for me."

Brody's face contorted playfully in confusion. "What's that mean?"

The woman lifted the tom, cradling it in her arms. "A cat's personality reflects the human they are with at any particular moment. Therefore, that person should be able to name the cat."

"And you picked Rhodenbarr?"

"Wouldn't you? I mean, the only addendum to the rule is that since this is a mystery bookshop, the name has to be from a mystery protagonist. Rhodenbarr seemed a natural choice."

"Naturally," Brody said, agreeing with the oddly cute woman even though he had no idea what she just said. "Who created this naming rule?"

"Why Alice, of course. This *is* her cat."

"And who is Alice?"

The woman eyed him suspiciously. "The owner of the bookstore. *Your* boss."

He stared at her.

"Alice Walker?" the woman said.

Brody shook his head.

The woman glanced around the shop. "Where *is* Alice?

He shrugged. "I own the bookstore now."

"Wait. What? Alice *sold* The Red Herring?" the woman said, confused. Her reaction caused the cat to jump from her arms and scamper into one of the aisles. She stepped to the counter. "How is that possible?"

"I bought it."

"Bought it?"

"Are we an echo?"

"I don't understand," the woman said. "She never mentioned wanting to do such a thing. Why would she do that?"

"I don't know."

"When?"

"What?"

"When did she sell it to you?"

"A few days ago, I guess."

The woman studied Brody for a moment then said, "I don't know about this."

"What don't you know?" Brody asked with a smile. The woman was disarmingly sweet.

"You don't look like the bookstore type."

"What do you mean?" he asked, feigning offense. "I like books."

"You do?"

"Yeah, sure," Brody said. "Agatha Christie is my favorite. I also like Sue Grafton and Janet Evanovich."

The woman crossed her arms and pursed her lips. "Well... you might be all right. *Maybe.*"

"Thank you," he confidently said.

Something fell in the back of the store, and Brody yelled, "Cat! Whatever you're doing, knock it off."

"Cat? That's the best name you could come up with?"

"Cut me some slack," Brody said with a slight grin. "I just learned about the naming rule. Until you showed up, I've had to survive by my own rules."

"Alice didn't tell you about the cat?"

Brody's smile faded. "No."

"That seems odd, doesn't it? To leave the cat with the store and not tell you about the naming rule? I'm surprised she would include the little guy with the purchase."

"I was surprised by it, too."

"Well," the woman said, glancing around the store as she thought, "give him a name. You can't go around calling a perfectly good cat, Cat. Only Audrey Hepburn can get away with that."

He stared at her.

"Holly Golightly? *Breakfast at Tiffany's?*" she said as if that jumble of five words would clear up the confusion.

Brody added a shrug and a head tilt to go along with his stare.

The woman rolled her eyes. "You need to come up with a name for the cat. Tell me, who is your favorite detective?"

Brody's gaze dropped to the counter where he saw MacDonald's book and its tagline *A Travis McGee novel*. He lifted his eyes to the woman and slowly said, "How about Travis?"

Her eyes twinkled. "Travis? Really?"

He nodded.

"As in Travis McGee?"

A car honked outside, and she turned to look. With her attention diverted, Brody swiped *The Deep Blue Good-by* off the counter, catching it with his foot so it wouldn't hit the floor and make a sound.

When the woman returned her focus to him, she leaned in and said, almost breathlessly, "Travis is a guilty pleasure of mine. He's sort of a misogynist, but don't you just love him?"

"I do," Brody said, "I do." At that moment, he really wished he knew who Travis McGee was.

She thrust out her hand and smiled. "I'm Daphne Winterbourne."

He carefully held her hand and introduced himself. "Brody Steele."

"Like Danielle?" she muttered as she focused on the tattoo covering the back of his hand. She examined the inky ball of fire. Her free hand hovered above it as if to feel some imaginary heat.

Brody didn't know how to respond to her question, so he asked, "Where do you work, Daphne Winterbourne?"

She let go of his hand. "At the Pleasant Peasant, the grocery store up the street."

"And what do you do there?"

"I'm the bookkeeper."

"No kidding," he said. "I used to be a bookkeeper."

"Before owning a bookstore?"

"Right."

"That's funny."

"I believe someone thought it was."

"What?"

"What?" Brody repeated.

The woman leaned in. "Who is *someone*?"

"I'm working on that."

Daphne eyed the man behind the counter. "I need to get back. I'm on my break and wanted to get away for a few moments and see if Alice had reopened the store. I guess she did, or well, you did."

He nodded, trying not to smile like a goofy kid.

"It was nice to meet you, Mr. Steele."

"You as well, Mrs. ...?"

"Ms."

A sheepish grin appeared. "Ms. Winterbourne."

She nodded once before leaving, the little bell announcing her departure from the store. She paused outside the window, looked back at him, and waved good-bye. He returned the gesture.

The ocean's aroma and the humidity that snuck inside the bookstore no longer bothered him.

Maybe living in Pleasant Valley wouldn't be so bad after all.

Chapter 3

"Living in Pleasant Valley is going to be murder!" he yelled and smacked the polished metal table.

Surprisingly, the older man sitting across from him didn't even flinch.

They were seated in a windowless room in Quantico, Virginia. Technically, it was home to the Federal Bureau of Investigation's training academy, and this small room was explicitly used to train FBI agents on how to survive being tortured if ever taken hostage.

However, today it was an impromptu meeting place for one man to begin his new life in the United States Federal Witness Protection Program. Holding the meeting at the training base was due to an interagency favor.

Stifling a yawn, U.S. Marshal Theodore 'Ted' Onderdonk said, "You're going to be fine."

"How can you possibly think that?" the big man asked.

Onderdonk leaned back in his chair, his eyes slowly blinking as if he were about to fall asleep. "Because I know it, Beau. This is what I do."

Beauregard 'Beau' Smith stroked his chest-length beard and studied the marshal. They'd only met a week ago, but his life was now in the hands of this cop. Onderdonk was in his late forties but appeared almost a decade older due to the lines on his tanned face. The salt and pepper mustache also aged the man. He wore a plaid short-sleeved shirt and khaki pants. His round badge was clipped to his belt, and a gun was on his hip.

"Are there even any valleys in Maine?"

"Of course, there are valleys in Maine, Beau. There are valleys everywhere. Don't be obtuse."

Beau's hand dropped from his beard and hit the metal table with a thud. He didn't like it when Onderdonk insulted him, and he especially didn't like it when the marshal used words that he barely understood. Beau glared at the man, but as usual, the marshal didn't care. Or he was good at faking that he didn't care. Either way, Beau respected Onderdonk for that. Most lawmen couldn't hide their emotions around him.

The marshal sucked something imaginary through his teeth before speaking again. "The town is on the edge of the ocean with its own bay. Right across from New Hampshire. You're going to love it." Onderdonk didn't sound convincing.

"I'm going to hate it," Beau said, reaching for the black cloth hoodie that lay on the metal table. He'd been required to wear it as a team of marshals escorted him onto the training facility and then into the room. Onderdonk didn't want anyone to see him arriving, even if they were a bunch of FBI recruits.

"You haven't given Maine a chance," the marshal said. "Don't be such a wimp."

Until very recently, no one would have dared call him anything close to that since he held the exalted position of bookkeeper for the Satan's Dawgs Motorcycle Club (MC). As with everything in the Dawgs, members in positions of power were given coded titles to make their activities sound legitimate in case their phones were tapped, or conversations were somehow overheard.

Beau Smith was its bookkeeper, which meant he was responsible for 'keeping book' on those who had crossed the club and for eventually settling those debts. He was very good at 'clearing the books,' and there was a long line of dead men to prove it. Because of his skills, he had been given all the rewards that came with it. Smith had his choice of the most beautiful women, the coolest bikes, the deadliest guns—the best of everything.

"No," Beau said. "This can't be happening. I filled out your forms. I talked with your headshrinkers. You're not supposed to put me in a small town. I'll get bored. I'll go crazy."

Onderdonk shrugged. "That's what the computer spit out. It runs complicated algorithms to figure out what's best for you. It's never wrong."

Beau slammed his fist against the table. "I. Don't. Care. Run it again."

Onderdonk held the back of his hand against his mouth as he yawned a second time. "It doesn't work like that, Beau. The computer reviews the data it's given, chews it up, and spits it out. Pleasant Valley, Maine is what it says you need for a safe, relaxing life."

"Relaxing? I don't want relaxing!" The big man jumped out of his seat, sending the metal chair spiraling behind him until it banged into the wall.

Beau walked back and forth, running his fingers through his long, dirty blonde hair while he thought. Finally, he turned and angrily pointed at the lawman. "It was Ekleberry, wasn't it?"

Special Agent Maxwell Ekleberry was the man who got Beau Smith, feared bookkeeper, to turn against his own club. The FBI agent had discovered the only thing Beau loved and used it against him.

Onderdonk shook his head. "Max doesn't have the juice to mess with the system. No one does. That's why it's the system."

Beau's eyes flattened. "Ted, someone always has the juice to mess with the system. You figure out the weak point and apply the appropriate pressure. Do I have to remind you why I'm here?"

"I get it, Beau. You're not happy with the assignment, but this is what we've got. Unless you want to sit in this box for the rest of your life."

The big man threw up his hands. "Fine. I'll stay here. It's gotta be better than Maine."

Onderdonk leaned back in his chair again. "For such a tough guy, you sure throw a temper tantrum when you don't get your way."

Beau scowled at the marshal, who smiled in return.

"Ever been to Maine?" Onderdonk asked.

He crossed his arms and leaned into a corner. "That's what I thought."

Beau looked away and stared at the bare, beige wall.

"How will you know you won't like it?"

"I won't."

"You sound like a child."

Beau pushed off the wall and stepped toward the table. "You calling me immature?"

"I'm calling you bratty."

That stopped the former bookkeeper. "Bratty?"

"As a twelve-year-old girl."

Beau shook his head. Only Onderdonk could get away with talking to him like that. A lot of it had to do with how the lawman playfully smirked as he verbally jabbed at him. It was a disarming trait that Beau weirdly admired. It's what kept Onderdonk's nose in place and his mouth full of teeth.

"What I'm saying is give it a chance, Beau. What do you have to lose?"

"My life."

"You're not going to lose your life, especially in Pleasant Valley, Maine. Besides, I'm good at what I do. As long as I'm assigned to be your witness inspector, you're in the best hands the agency has. I've never lost anybody as long as they've followed the agency protocols."

"The heck does that mean?"

"It means do what I say, and you'll stay alive."

"The whole MC is after me because of what I did for Ekleberry. Now, I've got to trust you to stay alive?" He shook his head in disgust. "The system is rigged."

"Of course, it is," Onderdonk agreed. "So is Las Vegas, but I bet you've put your money on the tables in hopes of beating them the same way you tried to beat the U.S. Government."

Beau thought about Vegas. He had gone there on yearly runs with the club from their home base in Phoenix, Arizona. While there, Beau would bet on all sorts of things. He knew those games were rigged and wasn't afraid to play. He also knew life was a rigged game. None of us were getting out alive. What mattered was how we showed up.

He picked up his chair and sat at the table. "What am I supposed to do in this town? Pleasant Valley, right? Do I have some sort of cover? Do I have a job?"

Onderdonk slid a file to him. "We have two days to get you ready."

"Two days? That's all?"

"It's enough. You're going to get a crash course on being a citizen."

"What am I going to do?"

"One of the businesses we own had a change in ownership. We'll install you as the new proprietor. Just tell people you bought it on the Internet."

"The Internet?"

"People sell businesses that way now. Easy peasy."

"Wait. The U.S. Marshals own businesses?"

"Of course, we do—hundreds of them. We use them for cover. And you're going to run one of them for us. Congratulations, Beau, you're now a top-secret employee of the U.S. government."

"Ugh," he said, opening the file. "So, what's my job?"

"You're going to run a bookstore."

"A *what*?"

"A bookstore. A mystery bookstore to be exact."

Beau blinked several times before asking, "Why would the computer think I would want to run a bookstore? I hate reading."

"You hate reading?"

"I haven't read a book since high school."

Onderdonk pulled the folder back to him while his eyes remained locked on Beau's. Slowly, he lowered his attention to the file and flipped to the original information sheet. "Huh," the lawman eventually said, his finger resting somewhere in the middle of the page.

"What?" Beau asked, pulling the file back to himself. In the former employment box, Beau had written *bookkeeper*. "Bookstore," he said. "Very funny."

"It's not supposed to be funny," Onderdonk said, once again pulling the file back to him. The marshal's voice became grave, and his eyes hardened. "This is supposed to be serious."

"What's wrong, Ted?"

The lawman leaned over the file, reading intently. "Something is wrong. Very wrong."

"How do you mean?"

"You shouldn't have been assigned to anything with a similar title to your previous... uh, occupation. We're supposed to ensure you sever ties with your old life, not give clues for people to locate you. We want to make it impossible for anyone to find you."

Beau stroked his beard as he listened to the marshal. He couldn't tell if the lawman was being serious or shining him on. Something in Onderdonk's tone had changed, and Beau couldn't put his finger on it.

"Even your new name is all wrong," the marshal muttered.

"What's my new name?"

The lawman pressed his finger onto the page. "Brody Steele, with an e at the end."

Beau leaned back, grinning. "Brody Steele. Not bad. It makes me sounds like an action movie star."

Onderdonk slapped the table, causing Beau to jump.

"That's a problem, don't you see? Your name is supposed to be boring. Something that people won't think twice about nor remember. Like Beau Smith."

"You're saying my name is boring?"

"Frankly, yeah."

"My name is not boring."

"Is Beau Bridges the cool brother?"

He smirked.

"And we're not supposed to use the same initials. BS."

"That sounds like BS."

Onderdonk's eyes slanted for a moment then eased. He returned to studying the file. "It's all wrong."

"So maybe Ekleberry *did* do it."

The marshal's lips twisted into a smirk. "No, Ekleberry did not do it. The man doesn't have that much pull to mess with the system. Besides, he's a ding-dong."

"But you think something happened."

The marshal nodded. "Yeah. I do."

"And you'll look into it?"

"You know I will."

Beau brightened. "So, I don't have to go to Pleasant Valley then?"

Onderdonk looked up from the file with a confused look. "What? No. You most definitely have to go."

"Why?"

"We have to figure out what's going on."

"Are you kidding? Maybe I'm being set up."

Onderdonk closed the file and pushed it to the side. "How will we know if you don't go? If we pull back now and announce someone screwed with this system, we're going to send a signal to whoever might be behind it all. We'll never find the truth. We're not going to be any better off than we are now."

"But I'll be safer."

The lawman dismissed him with a wave. "You're safe, Beau. Besides, nothing ever happens in Pleasant Valley. I've already told you that. You'll be fine. Just pay attention and keep your eyes open. I'll be in touch every few days."

The way Onderdonk quickly ended the conversation bothered Beau. Something wasn't right with the marshal. He seemed antsy and anxious. He might be a federal jerk, but he was his federal jerk. This man's job was to protect him, and he was trying to learn to trust him, but it seemed like Onderdonk was now rushing Beau into Pleasant Valley. Until that moment, he thought the lawman was on his side. Now, he wasn't sure.

Weirdly, though, that did it for Beau. He would go to Pleasant Valley. Not because Onderdonk said so, but because he didn't like people messing with his life. Besides, he wanted to know what was going on.

"Pleasant Valley, it is." The big man leaned back in his seat, tugging at his beard. "What else do I need to know before we get started?"

Onderdonk appraised Beau. "You need some new clothes."

"What's wrong with my clothes?"

"Pleasant Valley is a nice place with respectable people. You can't look like a thug. You need to look like a citizen."

"Okay, then. I'll buy a new shirt."

"No. You need a whole new wardrobe. The type of stuff you've never worn before."

The way the marshal said it left no room for negotiation. "Who's picking my clothes?"

"I am."

"Ugh," Beau grunted. If there was such a thing, Onderdonk looked like a fashion model for Dockers Over 50TM. He pulled on his beard and frowned.

The lawman smiled. "And we need to cut off that scraggly mess you call a beard."

"What?" Beau said, smacking the table. "No! The beard stays."

"It makes you look like a pirate."

"What if we cut it short?"

"Then you'll look like a hipster. No."

Beau tugged on his beard. "It gives me power. Like that guy in the bible."

"Speaking of that rat nest, your hair is coming off as well."

"You gotta be kidding me," Beau said, running his fingers through his long mane. "I'm never letting you cut my hair."

"Time to grow up," Onderdonk said. "You won't even know it's gone."

Chapter 4

Brody stared at himself in the restroom mirror, not recognizing the man reflected at him.

He looked like a salesman.

No, he decided, he looked like a government hack.

Worse, he sighed. He looked like a mystery bookstore owner.

His shoulders slumped. Brody ran his fingers through his businessman's haircut, then his tattooed hand touched his clean-shaven face. Next, he leaned in and examined his blue eyes. At least those were the same, he thought.

Well, they *looked* the same. Brody was starting to doubt himself.

He clicked off the light, stepped out of the bathroom, and moved to the front of the store. For a brief second, he thought he smelled the aroma of the ocean and felt a rise in humidity. He suddenly stopped when he saw the man leaning casually on the front counter.

Brody balled up his fists. "Ekleberry," he muttered.

Special Agent Maxwell Ekleberry looked more like a Texas Ranger than an FBI man. He stood almost six feet tall, but his dirty cowboy hat and scuffed leather boots made him seem much taller. He wore a faded western shirt and dusty blue jeans. His gun and badge were noticeably absent from his hip, but there were wear marks at their usual positions. Brody imagined Ekleberry's pick-up was parked somewhere not far from the store. The agent's vehicle was much newer than the rust bucket the marshal service had provided Brody.

Ekleberry removed an unlit match from his mouth. "Nice place. You must be a real hit with the geriatric crowd."

Brody looked at the front door. "How'd you get in here without ringing the bell?"

The FBI man shrugged. "Tricks of the trade."

"The same tricks you pulled to get me into this town?"

Ekleberry put the match back into his mouth, tucking it to the side. "Ted said you were prickly about being sent here."

"You talked with him?"

"I did."

"Why?"

"Because I worry about you, Beau."

"It's Brody now."

The G-Man snorted, barely containing a laugh. "I love the way you say that. It sounds like you're a kid from 90210."

"Don't mess with this cover and get me killed, Ekleberry."

"I'm not going to mess with it, *Brody*." He chuckled after saying the new name. "I also didn't send you here. Onderdonk said you accused me of doing so. It's not nice to accuse people of things unless you have proof."

The orange cat made an appearance then but stopped at the edge of the *Cozy* aisle to stare at the federal agent. He didn't come any farther into the shop. Instead, he gave the man in the cowboy hat a wide berth. Ekleberry noticed the tom and smirked.

"Didn't figure you to be a cat person."

"I'm not."

"What's its name?"

"Travis."

The special agent sniffed dismissively. "That's stupid."

While Ted Onderdonk had a way about him Brody weirdly respected, he did not feel that way toward the G-Man. The man had never been cruel, unfair, or dirty toward him, but Brody disliked him intensely. Mostly, it was because Ekleberry had jammed him up, and the big man would never forget it. There was always an underlying tension in his conversations with the agent. "Why are you here, Ekleberry?"

"To check on you."

"But you're not supposed to be here. Your part is done. You already ruined my life."

"Maybe I wanted to visit this town and see how you were getting along."

"Bull," Brody said.

The agent shook his head. "You're the only felon I've ever met who doesn't swear."

"My grandmother raised me to be a good man."

"Who kills people."

"I only killed those who deserved it."

"You deemed them worthy of killing because they crossed the club."

Brody shrugged. "I had standards for my work, which is more than most people can say. And you and the judge didn't put much value on those men I put in the ground because you traded their lives for information to go after my crew."

"A fat lot of good that did."

"I can't help it if your team couldn't build a better case. I held up my end of the bargain."

"I did, too."

Ekleberry had indeed kept his word. When the agency wanted to renege on their deal, Ekleberry made sure everybody stayed true to the agreement. He did his job, but that didn't mean Brody had to like the man. His eyes narrowed as he tried to intimidate the lawman.

The agent waved him off and said, "C'mon, Beau, gimme a swear word."

The store owner's glare faded. "It's Brody and no. I won't do that."

"C'mon."

"It's the sign of a weak mind, Ekleberry."

"Well, I swear," the agent flatly said.

"I know you do, but you're not going to do it here. Within these four walls, I make the rules."

"You can't stop me from doing it."

Without warning, Brody punched the federal agent, knocking his hat off. The man immediately brought his hands up to his face to cover his mouth.

"Want to arrest me?" Brody asked.

Ekleberry kept his eyes on the bigger man as he bent over to retrieve his hat. He smacked it against the side of his leg before placing it back on his head. "You ever do that—"

Brody punched him again, although this time, Ekleberry jerked his head at the last second, reducing its impact. The punch still hit the agent, and he stumbled several feet backward until he bumped into the book spinner.

"What the hell?"

"Please arrest me," Brody said, pushing his hands out in front of himself as if he was ready to be handcuffed. "Of course, you'll have to explain to Onderdonk why you're here. Maybe then he'll move me to another town."

The agent rubbed his hand over his mouth before saying, "I really was just checking on you."

Brody moved behind the counter and crossed his arms. The two men stared at each other for several unpleasant moments.

Finally, the big man asked. "Are you going to buy something?"

Ekleberry's eyes swept across the store. "Nope... I don't read."

Brody shook his head. "That's pitiful."

The G-Man pointed at him. "Watch it."

That made him smile.

Ekleberry stepped back and adjusted the waist of his jeans. "Maybe I should stop in and check on that grandmother of yours."

Brody's smile faded. "You leave her alone, Ekleberry. You've checked on her enough."

The federal agent chuckled as he walked to the door. "See you around, *Brody*."

When he stepped outside, Ekleberry looked back through the store's window. He then began yelling a series of expletives. Brody rolled his eyes. He wasn't going to invest any further energy in the agent.

A group of people strolled by and watched as Ekleberry turned red-faced while loudly cursing at the store.

Finally, the FBI man ran out of steam, glanced around, and walked off.

Chapter 5

It was shortly after 2 p.m., and Brody hoped no one else would come in for the day.

After Ekleberry's vulgarity-laced tantrum, Brody wanted to be alone and not be interrupted. He'd already had three visitors today, and two of them he could have done without.

He picked up *The Deep Blue Good-by* and struggled to get through the first couple of chapters.

He wasn't lying when he told the older woman he hadn't read a book since high school, almost twenty years ago. Brody knew most of the words, of course, but keeping his attention focused on a story was hard. He ached to get up and do something else.

Brody stayed with the book for one reason—he wanted something to talk with Daphne Winterbourne about the next time he saw her. She seemed excited about Travis McGee, so he persisted until his stomach told him he needed to find nourishment.

No one came into The Red Herring while he read the book, so he figured it didn't matter if he closed the store or not. Besides, the U.S. Marshals would ensure the business stayed operational. Selling books was optional since it was only a cover. He only had to *pretend* to sell them.

Brody locked the store and walked down Main Street as the summer sun pulsated down on the city.

He crossed the street and saw Pleasant Valley Sundae, the town's ice cream parlor, full of families. Even outside, he could hear the joyful ruckus caused by a building swarming with children. Brody wasn't in the mood for sweets, and he didn't want to be around kids. He enjoyed them about as much as he liked catching a social disease.

Several older women beamed at him as they passed. At first, he didn't know how to react. Strangers hadn't smiled at him since he was a little boy. By the time he was in high school, he'd gotten in trouble with the law and had a rough look that went along with that. Strangers would no longer smile when he passed by. Instead, they tended to frown and disapprovingly shake their heads.

Maybe it was the shoulder-length hair he'd grown or the black, heavy-metal T-shirts he wore with band names like Megadeth or Hellhammer. As he grew older, he developed a look befitting his reputation as a wild man—scruffy beard, long hair, and muscles from lifting weights.

When he joined the motorcycle club, he exchanged the heavy metal T-shirts for a Satan's Dawgs' leather vest. By then, strangers completely averted their eyes or crossed the street when he neared them. He liked the reverence that fear of the Satan's Dawgs had brought.

But not in Pleasant Valley, Maine. Here, everyone smiled at him.

He was surprised by how that simple act from others made him feel.

"Good afternoon," a silver-haired man said as he walked along, holding his wife's hand.

"Afternoon," Brody said hesitantly.

He stopped and watched the couple walk happily by. It felt weird to engage with everyday folks, *citizens* as the MC called them. It seemed so *normal*, something he believed only existed on television. A small grin crept on his face as he touched his short hair before rubbing his bare chin. Maybe looking like a bookstore owner wasn't so bad after all.

Brody continued down Main Street passing a salon (Pleasantly Pampered), a barbershop (The Valley Cut), and a dog groomer (Your Pleasant Pooch). He walked to the end of the street which served as cul-de-sac parking lot for the lighthouse. The tall white structure stoically stood guard over the harbor. He breathed in the ocean air for a moment and enjoyed watching the waves rush onto the beach and then slowly recede.

No one looked his way and, if they happened to glance at him, they didn't stay focused on him for long. Not because they feared him, but out of respect for his privacy. They were merely polite.

Maybe the computer had been right in selecting this little town for him to start a new life. It might have been small and boring, but he didn't feel watched, didn't feel hunted, and didn't feel the need to be hyperalert at every moment. An unseen weight began lifting from his shoulders, and he felt suddenly alive.

The humidity seemed thicker along the ocean, and the big man pulled the plaid shirt away from his skin. It was already sticking to him with sweat, and he'd only walked a handful of blocks.

His stomach rumbled again, and he turned back up Main Street, crossing to the other sidewalk. He knew there was an Italian restaurant in town (he saw it on his first drive through Pleasant Valley) and wanted to give it a try. It was two blocks up and to the right on Second Avenue.

Il Cuoco Irato was in a small brick building with a green, white, and red awning resembling the Italian flag. Brody pulled the door open and stepped inside. The first thing he noticed was the smell. It was a wonderful mixture of cooking meat, spices, and other scents he couldn't place.

A Frank Sinatra tune played softly in the background. It only took a moment for him to realize it was "The Best is Yet to Come." His grandmother loved music from the early sixties and listened to it frequently on her record player.

Red leather booths lined one wall, and small tables with red-cushioned chairs sat in the middle of the restaurant.

Except for those occupying the only semi-circular booth in the far back corner, there were no other customers.

A heavyset man in his late fifties sat in the middle of the corner booth. He wore a red jogging suit with a white T-shirt. On either side of him sat a twenty-something blonde, each wearing a tight white top and a little captain's hat as if they'd just come in off a boat. The man was cooing in the ear of one of the girls as he made eye contact with Brody.

He sat at a small table near the windows. He pulled a folding menu from the condiment holder, which rested in the middle of the table and began the process of selecting his lunch.

From the kitchen, an older man appeared. He wore a white shirt and black slacks. His bald head gleamed as if it was recently shined with a rag.

"Can I get you?" he asked, his English clipped.

"Meatball sandwich to-go," Brody said, "and a side of Caprese salad."

The man scribbled onto his notepad and disappeared into the kitchen.

From the corner, one of the girls giggled, which caused Brody to glance in that direction. The heavyset man growled, "Mind your own business, bub."

Usually, he would have taken insult with the man's blunt statement, but he needed to blend in with the sleepy town. He quickly decided to let it go.

Brody lifted a hand in apology, his eyes searching for something to entertain him. On a nearby table, he noticed a recent edition of the *Union Leader*. Brody grabbed the newspaper, returned to his seat, and slowly read through it. Since he found most of the national news boring, he skipped over it. It was the same thing, year after year, regardless of who was in control of the White House.

In the local section, he read about the body of an unidentified woman found in Massabesic Lake. She had been shot in the back of the head and dumped somewhere upstream. The police described her as being in her early seventies but gave no further information. They were unable to get fingerprints as her fingers had been removed, so they were waiting for dental records.

Brody hung on to the last fact. The woman's fingers were missing, but her teeth remained. Whoever killed her was either in a hurry, or they didn't know what they were doing. Removing only the fingers would simply slow the identification of the woman. It wasn't going to stop the cops. They were too sophisticated. To truly make someone disappear would require far more work than snipping fingers and dumping a body into a lake.

The cops were asking the public to contact them if they had any information on the missing woman. Brody wondered how often citizens actually did that.

He continued to flip through the paper until he got to the *Sports* section. There was an unusual amount of coverage about the Boston Red Sox. He also noticed reporting on the New Hampshire Fisher Cats.

What the heck is a Fisher Cat? he wondered.

Then he stopped and reread where the ballclub was from—New Hampshire.

He flipped back to the front of the newspaper and discovered that the *Union Leader* was based out of Manchester, New Hampshire.

What is a New Hampshire paper doing here in Pleasant Valley, Maine? Brody thought.

They were on the border of New Hampshire, so perhaps this was the newspaper of choice for the locals.

The waiter returned with the order in a Styrofoam container. He handed it to Brody along with a handwritten receipt. Brody eyed it for a moment, reached into his pocket, and pulled out a small roll of one-hundred-dollar bills. He peeled off one and handed it to the waiter.

The older man stared at the bill. "Smaller?"

"That's all I've got," Brody said.

The waiter clicked his tongue in disapproval then walked to the man sitting in the corner. He spoke to him in Italian and laid the hundred-dollar bill on the table. The heavyset man leaned to look around the waiter and made eye contact with Brody, who apologetically shrugged in return.

The man reached into his pocket and pulled out a large wad of money. Both girls stared excitedly at the cash. The man licked his thumb once before he began counting out several bills. He tossed them onto the table for the waiter who picked them up and hurried to the cash register. The heavyset man wrapped the hundred-dollar bill around his wad of cash and stuffed it back into his pocket. He then returned to cooing in one of the girl's ears.

When the waiter gave Brody his change, he left a tip and grabbed his lunch. He didn't bother looking back.

He knew what kind of establishment this was.

Chapter 6

"You must be da new ownah I heard so much about," the police officer said. The man's accent was thick and nasally.

He stood with his feet shoulder-width apart and his thumbs tucked into his leather duty belt.

Brody had heard the bell tinkle and stepped out from one of the book aisles where he was cleaning up another of the cat's messes.

When he initially saw the police officer, he paused for a moment because that was his natural reaction when encountering an officer of the law. He then moved slowly toward the man, trying to make sense of him because he was unlike any cop he'd ever seen.

He wore blue tennis shoes, dark blue cargo shorts, and a white short-sleeve shirt. Over his left breast was pinned a silver badge. Above the right pocket was a stitched nametag that read *Farnsworth.*

The officer also wore a bicycle helmet strapped tightly under his chin. Even with a gun on his right hip and a radio attached to his left, he didn't present an authoritative figure. Instead, he seemed more like a security guard than law enforcement officer.

"Excuse me?" Brody said.

Farnsworth waggled his finger in a circle. "The bookstore. You the new ownah?"

"Oh, sure."

The officer stuck out his right hand. "Constable Emery Fahnsworth." His accent was so strong it seemed like he was mispronouncing his name.

Brody held out his hand, palm up, so the officer wouldn't see the tattoo on the back of it. "Brody Steele," he said.

They quickly shook hands. When they broke their clasp, Brody shoved his hands into the pockets of his khakis.

"Constable, is it?" Brody asked.

"Actually, I'm an officah of the law, duly commissioned by the great state of Maine, but I really like how constable rolls off the tongue." Farnsworth smiled. "It sounds nicah, don't you think?"

"Don't constables have less authority than an officer?"

"What?" Farnsworth's face scrunched in disbelief. "No."

"Okay."

"Do they?" the officer asked.

The big man shrugged. "I don't know. Just making conversation."

"I'll have to look into that."

Brody watched the officer. He had obviously stopped into the store for something more than a welcome-to-the-neighborhood discussion.

"You bought the store from Alice Walkah?"

"Word travels fast."

Farnsworth stepped further into the shop, his eyes scanning the bookshelves. "Daphne told me."

"You know Daphne?"

The officer moved toward the back aisles, checking for something. "Ayuh. She's my girlfriend."

Brody repeatedly blinked, taking in what the officer had just said.

"Magnum?" Farnsworth said as he hunched over as if searching for something. "Where you at, buddy?"

"Daphne's your girlfriend?" Brody carefully asked.

The officer straightened. "Well... she was," he said, his voice now filled with disappointment. "Where's the cat? Daphne said Alice left him with you."

"Was?"

"Huh?"

"Daphne *was* your girlfriend?"

"Ayuh, ayuh," he said as if he sucked in words instead of speaking them. "She broke up with me a few months back."

"I see."

Farnsworth spun around. "You do?" he asked, hurrying toward Brody. "What do you see?"

Brody's eyes widened. In his old life as the Dawg's bookkeeper, he would have told the silly-looking cop to step back from him and pound sand. Here in Pleasant Valley, though, he was trying to learn a new set of rules and to abide by

Onderdonk's guidance to not call attention to himself.

"I don't see anything."

"But you said you saw something." Farnsworth studied Brody's eyes. "In fact, you said, 'I see.' That's what you said, right? 'I see.'"

"That's what I said, but I was only being polite."

"Polite?"

Brody nodded.

The officer frowned. "That's too bad. I'm still trying to figure out why she broke up with me."

Maybe it's your little boy's clothes, Brody thought. *And your plastic hat.*

Farnsworth stepped back, and his eyes again swept over the store. "Did Alice tell you where she moved to?"

"Why would she do that?"

"She was well-liked around here, and folks are curious as to why she would leave Pleasant Valley so unexpectedly."

"She didn't tell me anything. I never actually talked with her, though. I bought the business online."

It was the story Onderdonk had given him for a plausible change in ownership. The marshals had taken care of all the paperwork making Brody Steele the new owner. If anyone bothered to check, they would see the sale documents were fully in order.

"About a month and a half ago," Farnsworth said, "she started closing her bookstore in the middle of the day, which wasn't like her. I stopped in one morning to ask if everything was okay. She said it was, but she didn't look that way. She looked sort of flushed and harried. Know what I mean?"

"Not really."

"She also seemed distracted. Like she was bothered that I was there. That also wasn't like her. She and I used to have some good talks."

"Maybe she didn't want people poking into her business."

"Here in PV, everyone is in everyone's business."

Brody frowned.

"One of the ladies in her knitting circle, Martha Cole, said she saw her in Manchestah a month ago."

"Manchester, New Hampshire?" Brody asked, thinking about the newspaper he'd read at the Italian restaurant.

Farnsworth scrunched his face and pulled back slightly as if Brody had asked something stupid. "Of course, it's in New Hampshah. Where do you think she saw her, Manchestah, England?"

"How far is Manchester from here?"

"Three hours," Farnsworth said.

"And Martha saw Alice *there*?"

"Wait," Farnsworth said, "that's three hours by bicycle. It's less than an hour by car."

"You've ridden your bicycle for three hours?"

"Ayuh, it's a wonderful experience."

"Does Daphne ride?"

"I wish," Farnsworth said, again looking at Brody as if he'd asked a stupid question. "I bought her a bike and everything. She didn't even wanna ride to York Harbah. We could have done that in twenty minutes."

Brody studied him. For a police officer, he was missing the most obvious clues.

"You live in Alice's old place, the one upstairs?"

Brody nodded.

"It's strange."

"What is?" the big man asked.

"She was a nice woman," Farnsworth said. "I would have thought she would have said good-bye to her friends. She'd been here almost forty years."

"Some people just want to leave and start a new life," Brody said.

"Ayuh, maybe," Farnsworth said. He glanced around one final time. "If you see Magnum, give him a ruffle for me."

Chapter 7

After closing the store for the day, Brody climbed the outside stairs to a one-bedroom apartment above his bookstore. There was only minimal furniture inside—a bed, a nightstand, and a kitchen table with two chairs.

He'd slept in the bed the previous night and made it when he got up. It was a habit he'd learned while incarcerated.

He wondered if Alice had taken the furniture with her or if the marshals had removed it. Onderdonk said someone would be by in the coming weeks to help him select new furniture. The lawman asked him to be patient, promising to outfit his apartment with something acceptable.

Brody didn't care, though. He'd had less than this when he spent time in juvenile hall, jail, or prison. He could live in this sparsely decorated apartment quite nicely.

For what he had now was something he didn't have in those other places. Freedom. And peace. In fact, he had neither when he was with the club. Someone was always watching him.

But no one watched him now.

Except maybe the Marshal Service, and they only wanted him to abide by a simple set of rules.

Do not contact people from your old life.
Do not visit places from your old life.

Do not develop habits from your old life.

He was to discard anything that had to do with Beau Smith. Only Brody Steele could survive now.

This whole mess, he had decided, was his doing. His actions and selfishness caused this life of loneliness, this life of hiding, this life in Pleasant Valley. Federal Agent Max Ekleberry might have been the architect, and Marshal Ted Onderdonk built the structure, but Brody laid the foundation for this life.

His house of cards began to fall when his grandmother ended up in financial problems. To get out of a bind, she mortgaged the house she had lived in for almost sixty years. Unfortunately, she fell behind on her payments and didn't tell Brody about her troubles until it was almost too late. She wasn't the type of woman to ask her grandson for aid. He only found out about her predicament when he visited and discovered the foreclosure documents on her dining room table.

Brody did the only thing he knew how to do—he went into action. At first, he threatened a bank officer. This only got him into trouble. Realizing too late that he couldn't bully his grandmother's problems away, he did what every citizen in the world must—he paid the bank what it was owed. Then he paid off the rest of her mortgage.

Afterward, Brody hired contractors to improve her home, fixing things that had gone unrepaired for years. It felt good to assist the woman he regarded as his true mother, the only person he had ever really loved.

Unfortunately, Ekleberry and his team had been watching the Satan's Dawgs. Brody's threatening of the bank officer had not gone unnoticed, and it led the FBI man to his grandmother. When the federal agent discovered Brody was using illegally gotten gains to not only pay off his grandmother's mortgage but to upgrade her house, he had found his leverage point.

Ekleberry approached Brody's grandmother and explained who and what her grandson indeed was. This shocked her as she had never known he was in a motorcycle club. She had always thought he was in a rock and roll band, just on the cusp of making it big. Every grandmother wants to believe her grandson will someday be rich and famous. The idea that her grandson was a criminal broke her heart. When the agent had her in his pocket, he met with Brody.

That's when the big man threatened to kill Ekleberry. It was yet another mistake Brody made along the way. The G-Man explained the U.S. Government was preparing to seize his grandmother's house due to his use of illegal funds to pay off its mortgage and to increase its value through improvements. They would argue that Brody had laundered money through his grandmother's home.

Brody wrongly claimed there was no proof of the illegality of those funds and then stated no one had been arrested. Therefore, he argued that the government could not go after his grandma's house. It was at that moment the FBI man read him his rights and put handcuffs on him.

The arrest of the remaining crew soon followed. Everyone was arraigned and assigned a lawyer, but the feds were really going after only one man that day—Beauregard Smith.

It didn't take long for Brody to roll on his brothers though. Partially it was because his grandmother asked him to do so, but there were other circumstances at play.

The club had stopped being the family he searched for when he was younger and was now a machine for greed. They were running drugs and guns and had gotten into a variety of deadly alliances around the country. His skills as a bookkeeper were recently lent out to other charters. What he did was for the club. It wasn't some sick service to be provided to others for whom he had no loyalty. Therefore, he had already been looking for a way out.

Even before their arrests, the brothers in the club were turning on one another. There was too much money at stake for loyalty to remain the most valuable thing. Brody believed the end was near when the current president began a systematic witch hunt of his own, demanding repeated loyalty oaths to himself followed by tests of faithfulness. He had already proven his faithfulness by being the bookkeeper. Jumping through hoops like a trained puppy wasn't something he would do.

Yet he did exactly that for the FBI and then the U.S. Marshals.

He lay on the bed and stared at the ceiling, listening to the occasional slow-moving car passing along Main Street. Now and then, a horn from a boat sounded in the bay. These were the sounds of his new life.

Admitting I like being here wouldn't make me less of a man, would it?

Besides, it was Brody Steele who liked the sounds and aromas of Pleasant Valley, not Beau Smith.

Brody Steele was also intrigued by the cute bookkeeper who worked at the grocery store. Beau Smith would never have known what to say to her, and she would never have given the rough biker the time of day.

Brody Steele had enjoyed the casual walk along Main Street with sweet, older people smiling at him. Beau Smith would never have experienced that.

But at the Italian restaurant, Il Cuoco Irato, it was Beau Smith who identified the true nature of the restaurant. For bookstore owner, Brody Steele, it would have been only a place that served a moderately good Caprese salad and a below-average meatball sandwich.

What should he do about the restaurant then?

Should he tell the police?

Or call U.S. Marshal Ted Onderdonk?

Or worse, should he notify FBI Special Agent Max Ekleberry?

No, Brody decided. He wouldn't tell anyone.

The motorcycle club's unofficial motto was Do Unto Others Before They Can Do Unto You.

Now he was going to survive by a new motto—Live and Let Live.

Except the club wasn't going to let him just live. They would never forget what he did. For immunity for his own crimes, he rolled on the club. A few guys went to prison, but most of them avoided a single day behind bars. Turning into a rat did one positive thing for the club though.

It galvanized them behind a single purpose.

The Satan's Dawgs were now solely focused on hunting Beau Smith, their former bookkeeper and once-loyal brother.

Brody Steele rolled over, closed his eyes, and went to sleep.

Chapter 8

In the morning, Brody showered and shaved, the latter of which still felt odd and awkward. He then dressed in yet another pair of khakis and a plaid shirt. Before his arrival in Pleasant Valley, Ted Onderdonk had purchased him seven pairs of tan pants and a different plaid button-up for each day of the week. At least the man had bought him different colored underwear. Not wearing black T-shirts, jeans, and boots felt weird. It had been his uniform for the last twenty years except for those times while he was in prison.

After leaving his apartment, he walked through the nearby neighborhood, checking out the houses that shared the alley with his bookstore.

On both sides of A Street, the houses were beautiful and well kept. Manicured lawns, each with a white picket fence, abutted the sidewalks. Many of the homes appeared to be recently painted. Brody slowed his gait, his eyes glancing to each side of the road, while he appreciated how nicely coordinated the colors of the houses seemed to be.

He did not grow up in a neighborhood like this. He'd never even seen a nice home until he'd burglarized one as a teenager. For a while, his mother dated a man who ran an automobile recycling yard, and they lived with him on-site in a rusting, single-wide trailer. That was his favorite home growing up, partly because he got to operate the car crusher as an eleven-year-old boy, and partially because he could disappear into the labyrinth of decaying cars waiting for their ultimate death.

In several of the yards he passed, silver-haired men tended to their small flower beds. They smiled and waved at Brody. He nodded and raised his hand in acknowledgment. He still couldn't get over how friendly people were to him due to the simple change in his appearance.

When he finished reconnoitering the neighborhood, Brody returned to Main Street. He was ready for some breakfast.

A Pleasant Meal, the small restaurant at the west end of Main Street, was packed. Cars filled the lot, and others were on the street. Brody pulled the door open and was met with not only the smell of frying bacon and eggs but a cacophony of voices.

Several people sat on chairs just inside the door. They looked up at him with both kindness and desperate hunger, silently begging him not to make them wait any longer than necessary.

A woman with a brown apron approached him. "About a twenty-minute wait, hon, unless you wanna sit at the bar."

"The bar is fine."

The stools at the counter were caramel-colored vinyl high-backs bolted to the floor. Brody sat in one and spun forward. From his position, he could see two men in the kitchen hurrying behind a large grill. Several waitresses moved quickly about the restaurant attending to the customers.

The waitress with the brown apron stepped behind the counter, slid a menu in front of Brody, and asked, "Like some coffee?"

"Black," he said, "and I'm ready to order."

She glanced at the unopened menu then pulled out her order book. "What's your choice?"

"Three scrambled eggs. Hash browns. Sausage links. You've got the links, right? Not the patties."

"No patties," she mumbled.

"Good. And no toast."

"Stayin' away from the carbs?"

"Carbs?"

The waitress looked up from her order book to quickly appraise the big man. "Never mind."

"And if you've got a banana, bring one of those, but don't peel it. I'll take it with me."

"Banana for the road," the waitress muttered. She then tapped her notepad once with her pen before stepping over to the men at the grill. She clipped Brody's order to a ticket wheel and wandered off.

He glanced at the elderly gentlemen who sat on either side of him. Each nodded politely and smiled. He did so in kind. For a moment, he allowed himself to get lost in thought.

I'm in Mayberry, he mused.

He remembered watching reruns of *The Andy Griffith Show* as a child while visiting his grandmother. Being with her was a magical place, and he wished she was his real mother. Instead, he had a train wreck of a mom who invited drama into her life as if it was an old friend. The turmoil started long before his father showed up and swept her off her feet. It would continue long after she named her first and only child after the handsome stranger who vanished in the night after stealing not only her heart but her car.

While he stayed with his grandmother, though, she encouraged him to watch wholesome programs like *The Andy Griffith Show*. Andy, Opie, and Aunt Bee painted a black and white picture of what a perfect American town was supposed to be. A wry smile pushed at his lips when he thought of Barney Fife and realized Constable Emery Farnsworth could fill that role quite nicely.

When he was a kid, he wanted to visit a place like Mayberry, and now he lived in the real deal. Maybe the U.S. Marshal's supercomputer did get it right, and no one messed with the system. Was this where Brody was truly meant to be?

A group of women suddenly laughed, and he turned in his chair to look at them. Seated at a table near the windows were seven silver-haired women. Each appeared to be in their seventies, and all of them were either knitting or crocheting. They were smiling and clearly enjoying themselves.

Brody stood and walked over to their table.

"Excuse me," he said.

The ladies all looked up. Not one of them stopped their hands from working while they watched him.

"Is there a craft store in town?"

Most murmured in affirmation, and one of the ladies nodded toward the woman with a short haircut. "Martha has a store."

The woman smiled while she continued to work her knitting needles.

"Martha Cole?" Brody asked.

Her hands stopped. "Why, yes. How did you know that?"

"I heard your name yesterday. From Officer, I mean Constable Farnsworth."

The women muttered their appreciation of the constable.

"Oh, Emery," Martha said. "Isn't he delightful?"

"Yes," Brody agreed. "Delightful."

The rest of the women purred in support of Emery's delightfulness.

"Martha, where is your store located?" Brody asked. "My grandmother taught me how to knit when I was young. Believe it or not, it's helped me whenever I've had to deal with," he paused for the right word, "downtime."

"Like when you were in the Navy?" one of the ladies inquired.

"Excuse me?" Brody asked.

"The Navy," she said, pointing to the flame tattoo on the back of his hand.

"Yes, ma'am," he lied. "I knitted while on the ship."

"Thank you for your service," several of the ladies said in unison. Several other tables looked his way then added their thanks for his service while in the military.

Brody rubbed his newly short hair. He'd never once been mistaken for a military man.

"My shop," Martha said, "is on Blue and Fourth."

"You know how to get around town?" another woman asked. "It can be very confusing."

Main Street divided the town. South of Main, the streets were labeled by letters. The city made it to E Street. To the north of Main, the streets were named after colors. There were only three: Blue, Yellow, and Red. The roads that ran east and west were called 'avenues' and started at the beach with First. The town made it to Seventh Avenue before petering out.

"It is confusing," Brody agreed, "but I think I have it almost figured out."

That seemed to please the women.

He turned to Martha. "I'll stop by later today. I find myself with a lot of free time right now. Getting back to knitting would probably be good for my soul."

"It most certainly would be," she said brightly.

Brody waved goodbye to the group and went back to the counter where his breakfast now waited.

The elderly man to his right said, "I almost ate your breakfast while you were ovah there flirtin' with the ladies, but I didn't wanna do that to no naval officah."

Brody resisted smiling and patted the older man on the back.

He had only just joined, yet he'd already been promoted in his pretend naval career.

Chapter 9

Brody looked up from the fifth chapter of *The Deep Blue Good-by* when the brass bell jingled.

Even though he wasn't much of a reader, he knew not to judge a book by its cover. However, he could immediately tell the man standing at the entrance did not belong in a bookstore.

He was overly tanned and weightlifter big, his white tank top stretching over his thick chest. Red workout pants strained around his thighs, a white stripe ran down the sides to extremely white tennis shoes, as if they had never been outside of the gym. His dark hair appeared wet and was combed straight back. A gold chain with a small gold barbell dangled around his neck.

Brody closed his book and set it on the counter.

The door closed behind the man, the bell tinkling once more as it did.

"You da new ownah?" he asked. His accent was thicker than Emery Farnsworth's and filled with cockiness.

"Looking for a book?"

The weightlifter smirked. "What kinda question is that?"

"This is a bookstore."

"You some kinda smaht guy?"

"Next to you."

The weightlifter paused, his smirk deepening. He was about to say something when the orange cat ambled out. Travis plopped himself down in the middle of the store and watched the stranger.

"What's his problem?"

"He doesn't have a problem."

"That's a weird lookin' cat," the weightlifter said. "Pfft. Go on."

Unfazed, the cat remained where he was.

"He must think you're Schwarzenegger."

The man's eyebrows rose briefly, then he bent over, reaching for the cat. A smile grew on his face. "Ya think so?"

"Totally," Brody said. "He wants to know how much you bench."

The cat bolted for a nearby aisle. The weightlifter slowly straightened, the smile melting from his face.

"If you're not here to buy a book," Brody said, "then what are you looking for?"

"I'm lookin' for you, smaht guy."

"Why's that?"

"Why do ya think?"

Brody shrugged. "Need a tutor?"

"Smaht. Real smaht."

"You said it."

"What are ya doin' here?" the weightlifter asked.

"Me? Trying to sell books, but I still don't know what you want."

The weightlifter twisted his lips and studied Brody. "I ain't buyin' it."

"If you're not buying, then take off. You're sucking up all the oxygen."

"What's that mean?"

"It means leave."

The weightlifter flicked *The Deep Blue Good-by* from the counter to the floor. "Nobody talks to me that way," he said.

Brody stepped around the counter to stand nose-to-nose with the man. "Looks like I'm talking to you that way."

"Tell me why you're here."

"I just got out of the Navy and bought a bookstore. What more do you need to know?"

The weightlifter stepped back, his eyes scanning him. "The Navy, huh?"

"Got a problem with that?"

He shook his head. "Nah. No problem. Thank ya for your service."

Brody nodded his appreciation. Enlisting for the imaginary service was turning out to be a great decision.

"How'd ya come by this business?" the weightlifter asked.

"I bought it. On the Internet."

"Ya did, huh?"

"I did."

"From who?"

"An attorney." Throwing an attorney into the mix, just like mentioning a cop, usually stalled any conversation with this type.

"What happened to the old ownah? The smaht-mouthed broad."

"No idea. I only worked with the lawyer." As an afterthought, Brody said, "Online."

The weightlifter smirked. "Yeah, all right, smaht guy, we got our eye on ya." He spun and sauntered out. The ocean's aroma and summer's humidity entered again.

Who the heck did he mean by we? Brody wondered.

Chapter 10

By mid-morning, Brody had read as much as he could take of Travis McGee. No other customers had stopped in the store, real or threatening. His boredom had reached the maximum threshold, yet he was a man who knew how to deal with that part of life. Prison had taught him that skill. Luckily, he did not need to deal with it here.

He wrote a note and taped it to the window. *Back in twenty minutes.* Then he locked up the store.

The Pleasant Peasant wasn't a typical grocery store found in most metropolitan cities. At most, the business was a third of that size. It didn't need to be much bigger than that to support Pleasant Valley. Even with the surge in the tourist season, it seemed as if the store was a bit big.

Nauseatingly cheerful Muzak played in the store, and bright fluorescent lights shone down to the shimmering tile floor. A couple of checkers stood behind their counters, helping customers.

Brody walked up to a young man with impeccably combed hair. A name tag clipped to his green apron read *Aaron.* When the checker finished ringing out his customer, he turned to Brody.

"Can I help you, sir?"

"Is Daphne available?"

"May I ask who you are?"

"I'm the guy asking for Daphne."

Aaron carefully appraised him, which caused Brody to scowl. He was quickly annoyed by the man's disapproving judgment.

The cashier stepped back and picked up a microphone that rested near the register. He pressed a red button, which resulted in an irritating squawk over the store's intercom system.

"Daphne," Aaron said, announcing her name throughout The Pleasant Peasant. "A man who won't identify himself is at the front counter and would like to talk with you."

Several patrons and the other cashier looked in his direction. A woman stepped into Aaron's line and watched the interaction between the two men with great curiosity. Brody's annoyance with the checker immediately turned to dislike.

"Was that necessary?" Brody asked.

"I think so since you won't tell me who you are."

"What business is it of yours?"

Aaron again pressed the microphone button and caused another screech through the store's intercom. "He still won't tell me who he is, Daphne."

Brody glanced at the patrons in the store. More customers were stepping out of the aisles to witness their interaction. It seemed that everyone was staring at him now.

"What is your problem?"

"Tell me your name, sir."

"No."

Aaron held up the microphone with his thumb over the red button. It was meant clearly as a threat.

Brody couldn't believe it. A grocery store clerk was harassing him. As the bookkeeper for the Satan's Dawgs, he would have made the register jockey eat the microphone by now. But as the owner of The Red Herring, he needed to be on his best behavior. This was for many reasons, not the least of which was hurrying down the middle aisle now.

Daphne Winterbourne called out, "Aaron! Leave him alone."

"He won't tell me his name."

"He's the new owner of The Red Herring."

Aaron lowered the microphone, his eyes full of distrust. "Why didn't you say so?"

When Daphne was near Brody, she smiled up at him. "Mr. Steele, what brings you to The Pleasant Peasant?"

"You do, Ms. Winterbourne."

"I do?"

Aaron leaned toward them as did the older woman still waiting for her groceries to be totaled.

Brody lightly touched Daphne's elbow and guided her to a quieter place. He saw the disappointment on both the faces of the checker and the aged customer.

"I came to ask you out... on a date," Brody slightly stammered.

"A date?" she muttered as she pushed her round glasses back up the bridge of her nose.

"Yes. Would you go to dinner with me?"

Daphne stepped back from him. "I barely know you, Mr. Steele."

"That's why we should have dinner together."

She carefully studied him as her eyes slanted with suspicion. "I don't know about this."

"What's not to know?"

"I'm still not sure about you and the bookstore."

"I don't understand."

"Alice Walker and I were friends. She wouldn't just leave town without saying goodbye. Then you show up, saying you own her store."

"Then let's go to dinner, and you can tell me about Alice. Maybe we can track her down together."

"But you bought her business. You should be able to get that information from whoever helped you."

Brody nodded. "I will try. As soon as I leave here, I'll work on tracking her down."

"Really?"

"Of course."

"Well, thank you, Mr. Steele."

"You're welcome, Ms. Winterbourne. About dinner? We can go anywhere. If you like, we can go out of town."

"Why would we do that? Pleasant Valley has everything I would ever want."

Brody blinked several times, not knowing quite how to respond to that statement.

Daphne studied him for several seconds. Finally, she said, "Mr. Steele, if you want to take me out to dinner, you can take me to the new Italian restaurant."

"Il Cuoco Irato?"

"Then, you've seen it?"

"Yeah."

"Do you like Italian?"

Except for when it's a bodybuilder that walks into my store. "It's new?"

"A few months, maybe a little more. Everyone is talking about it, but I haven't been there yet. I've been waiting for something special."

"And this will be special?"

Daphne's smile was bright. "Won't it be?"

"I hope so." He grinned.

"Then I will meet you there at seven."

"Meet me? Can't we walk there together," Brody said. "Or do you live far?"

"Oh, no, I live in town, but walking together seems too forward for a first date. Don't you think? No, I'll meet you there."

Brody almost laughed. Walking together would be too forward for a first date. Daphne Winterbourne was like a woman from another planet. She was different from any woman he'd ever met.

"Fine," Brody said. "Seven, it is."

"See you then." She turned and headed toward the back of the store. Brody kept waiting for her to turn around and see him watching. When she didn't, he was slightly disappointed.

He noticed Aaron watching him, though. A malevolent grin grew on the cashier's face.

"I'll make sure to let her know you stayed until she made it to the back."

Brody pointed at the clerk and thought about saying something threatening. Instead, he waved it off in frustration. He didn't need the entire store to know about it.

Chapter 11

Brody walked over to Blue Street to find What's the Point?, Pleasant Valley's only craft store.

The business was in a converted house painted in pastel colors. He ascended the stairs, stepped inside, and was greeted with the sound of a rain forest. He searched around until he found a little noise machine next to a table-top water feature.

Martha Cole stepped around the counter, a smile broadening her already round face. Her hair was curly, and she wore a loose-fitting shirt with large bell sleeves.

"I was hoping you'd come in," she said, approaching him with her right hand out.

Brody shook her hand, and Martha clasped it with both of hers.

"It's so nice to have someone new in our town," she said. "Where were you before this?"

"Leavenworth," he said.

Martha held a finger to her chin as she thought. "Isn't that in Kansas?"

"Yes, ma'am."

"There's a naval base there? It seems odd in the middle of the country, so far from the ocean."

"I was recruiting," Brody lied. It was easier than telling her that he was being held in the federal prison there.

"Oh, my," she said, patting his hand. "This must be quite the culture shock then. Midwest to the east coast."

"It is," Brody said. "Definitely."

"How long were you stationed there?"

"Just a short time," Brody said.

"You don't stay in one place for very long, do you?"

"I've been a vagabond recently, that's for sure."

Martha's smile was kind and motherly. "You said your grandmother taught you how to crochet?"

Brody shook his head. "No, she taught me how to knit."

"That's right. And you did it while on ship?"

He lied by nodding.

The guys in the MC thought Brody's knitting was a weird habit since he only did it after he cleared the book on someone. Once the guys realized it was his special kind of therapy, they left him alone. Everyone had a type of release after doing dirty work. Some guys self-medicated by drinking or doing drugs. Others cavorted with women. Some even harmed themselves. Brody knitted.

He even taught one of the club's girls how to do it. She eventually created a shawl for her mother.

Most of the time, Brody would knit for a while, then pull the rows of stitches apart, rewrap the yarn, and put it away. While he was with the club, he never created a finished product. It was the simple act of knitting that calmed his mind.

"So, what can I do for you?" Martha asked.

"I need a kit," Brody said. "Needles, yarn, a bag. Something basic. I have nothing with me."

Martha's face lit up. "Fantastic!" She buzzed around the store, holding up items for Brody's approval, to which he always nodded acceptance.

"Martha?" Brody said.

"Hmmm?" Martha was in the process of selecting a yellow yarn for Brody.

"You knew Alice Walker, right?"

"Of course, dear. She was in our knitting circle. Why do you ask?"

"I'm the new owner of the bookstore."

Martha straightened, a look of surprise on her face. "You are?"

"I am."

"What happened to Alice?" Martha asked.

"I don't know."

"What do you mean you don't know? How did you come by the bookstore?"

"She sold it to me."

"She sold it to you, but you don't know what happened to her? None of us knew she was even considering such a thing."

"All I know is she sold it to me through an online company, but everyone I've come into contact with so far has said she loved the store."

"She did. It was her passion."

"See what I mean? Do you know if she was sick?"

Martha tilted her head. "What do you mean?"

"Constable Farnsworth said you saw her in Manchester a month ago. I thought maybe she was going to the hospital over there."

"I did see her, but she didn't seem sick. At least, she didn't look that way."

"What was she doing in Manchester then?"

"I don't know, but she was with a man."

"Like on a date?"

"I doubt that. At first, I thought it might be the foreign man she'd talked about, but he was much youngah than I expected."

"She was seeing someone?"

"Alice let it slip at one of our circles that she was seeing a handsome foreignah."

"Did she say where he was from?"

"Oh, no. Alice was very private. When she let that little nugget of information slip, she didn't say much more than that. It was very unlike her to share personal information. She lived her life by the motto of Loose Lips Sink Ships. You, being a navy man and all, should appreciate that."

"I do. Trust me. What did the man look like? The one she was with while in Manchester."

She thought about it for a moment, and then her eyes looked Brody up and down. "I would say he looked a lot like you."

"Like me?"

"Not exactly like you. Older and smaller, but he dressed a lot like you, except I think his shirt had short sleeves."

"He wore khakis and a plaid shirt?"

"Ayuh, ayuh," she said, inhaling her affirmations.

There had to be a lot of men in the world dressed in plaid shirts and khaki pants, but Brody only knew one other man. Ted Onderdonk. Since The Red Herring was a U.S. Marshal cover and Alice Walker was the previous owner, it wasn't hard to connect the dots to Onderdonk.

"How did Alice look when she was with this man?"

Martha paused. "I would say she looked like her normal self."

"Did you say hello to her while in Manchester?"

"No. I was in my car, and she was crossing the street. She didn't see me."

Brody fell silent then.

"But when she came home, I—"

"You saw her back in town after that?"

"Oh, sure. When she came home, I asked her what she was doing in Manchestah. She said she had never gone there. I thought that was strange, but she swore she was nevah there."

"Did you believe her?"

"I did. I thought maybe I was mistaken. Then she disappeared, and I thought maybe I really did see her, and something was wrong."

"How long has she been gone?"

"Maybe three weeks now."

"You told this to the constable, right? What did he do?"

"He looked into it."

"And what did he say?"

Even though they were the only two in the store, Martha leaned in and whispered, "Emery is a dear boy, but he isn't the most accomplished constable."

"Did anyone else in the department know about it?"

"There are only two people in the Pleasant Valley police department. Emery and the chief. And the chief, well, he's less accomplished than Emery."

"Emery could have called for outside help."

"I don't know if he did that. You'll have to ask him. Why are you so interested in Alice?"

Brody shrugged. "It seems weird for her to leave so suddenly if she loved the town and her business."

Martha laid the supplies she had collected onto the counter. "She did love it here."

"How long did she live in town?"

"She moved here in the early eighties. Right about the time Ronnie was voted president. Those were great times."

"Was the bookstore opened before then?"

"Ayuh, it was. It was a metaphysical bookstore before then, but Alice wouldn't go for any of that nonsense. She didn't believe in that mystical mumbo jumbo."

"She'd been here for almost forty years, running a bookstore?"

"Ayuh," Martha said, ringing up the items on the cash register.

"So, one day, she doesn't open the store and leaves her cat behind?"

"Alice left Wallander?"

"She did. Do you want him?"

"Oh no," she said. "Every bookstore needs a cat, don't ya know?"

"I've been told."

Martha announced the total cost, and she placed the various items in a bag.

After paying, Brody asked, "Do you miss her?"

"Of course, I do, but she tended to keep to herself. Even when she participated in our knitting group, she never talked much. I've known her for almost forty years, and I couldn't tell you where she came from or anything about her family. It's funny how people are. I've known you one day, and I already know you were in the Navy and just moved here from Leavenworth, and your grandmother taught you to knit."

Brody grabbed the bag and winked at her. "I'm an open book that way, Martha."

Chapter 12

When he returned to the bookstore, he tore down his handwritten back soon sign, tossed his knitting kit on the counter, and picked up the store's telephone. He dialed a number he had recently committed to memory.

A friendly female voice answered. "Ace Adventures, where your next journey begins. How may I help you?"

Somewhere the phone number he was calling from was already being traced, pinpointing his exact location.

"This is Brody Steele. I'm already a customer of yours."

From over the phone, he could hear her clicking on the keyboard. "Yes, I see it right here. Good morning, Mr. Steele. How may I help you?"

"I need to speak with Mr. Onderdonk."

More keyboard clicking.

"Is there a problem with your current vacation rental?"

Brody smirked. The U.S. Marshals went to great length to protect their witnesses. The bogus adventure agency was just in case another pair of ears was listening. Unfortunately, it made the process of getting to Onderdonk a pain in the butt.

"Yeah," Brody said. "My current rental is infested with bugs."

"Real bugs?" The woman immediately realized what she said and continued. "Of course, they're real. I'm sorry I implied anything else." The keyboard clicking was sporadic as she spoke. "What kind of bugs do you think they are?"

"The big Italian kind."

There was a long pause.

Finally, the woman said, "I'll have Mr. Onderdonk check in with you shortly."

"Thank you," Brody said and hung up.

***

Thirty minutes later, he looked up from the row of stitches he'd just knitted. The bell was still swinging, its high-pitch tinkle fading after the woman entered. She was tall, thin, and platinum blonde. Her hair looked professionally done, as did her breasts. She wore a blue Polo shirt, white shorts, and white sandals. Her perfect tan was earned elsewhere, likely in a spray booth.

Behind her shuffled a teenaged girl who wore a black T-shirt, black jeans, and black Vans. Her black hair was cut short, and her black eyeliner was heavily applied.

Brody set the knitting needles and yarn on the counter and watched the two.

Travis ambled over to check on the new visitors. He stopped, assessed them both, and moved toward the girl.

The woman frowned at the cat before appraising Brody. She lifted her eyebrows with what appeared to be appreciation and stepped to the counter.

"What's the cat's name?" she asked. Her smile was overly inviting while her eyes were penetrating.

"You decide."

"How's that?" Her smile never wavered, but her eyes bore deeper into Brody.

"Supposedly, a cat reflects a human's personality or some nonsense. So, when you're with the cat, you get to name him, but it has to be a mystery professional."

Her eyes relaxed, and her lips parted slightly. "That's cute," the woman almost whispered. "Whatever it means." She rested her hand on the counter near Brody's. He noticed the extraordinarily big diamond on her wedding ring.

"A mystery professional?" the teenager chimed in as she knelt and studied the cat.

Brody nodded. "Yeah, that's part of the rule."

"Did you create that rule?" the woman asked.

"The store's previous owner did."

The girl looked up to Brody as the cat slowly turned in circles for her. "What's a mystery professional?"

"It's the star of the book."

The teenager smiled knowingly then. "You mean the protagonist."

The woman rolled her eyes. "Miss Smahty-Pants ovah there."

"I think she's right," Brody said. He repeated the word, "Protagonist," trying to stick it to memory.

The girl stood and moved deeper into the bookstore. Travis followed her.

"She's always right," the woman whispered. "It bothahs me."

"Why?"

"She ain't my kid. She's my husband's. From the first wife."

"Oh."

"I'm his third," the woman said, touching the ink on Brody's hand. "Were you in the military?"

He pulled back slightly. "The Navy," he muttered.

"From ovah in Portsmouth?" she asked. The way she asked made him worried she might have some familiarity with the nearby base.

Brody shook his head. He once saw a naval shipyard in Southern California while on a run with the Dawgs. Brody figured he should say that base since it was the furthest away he knew. "San Diego," he lied.

The woman leaned back and assessed him. She glanced around even though it was just the two of them now and said, "Oh my God, you were a Navy SEAL, weren't you?"

"What?" Brody said. "No." His imaginary enlistment was getting out of control.

She leaned back in and whispered, "I once dated a SEAL, and you look sorta like him. Big and handsome, I mean. He nevah talked about it eithah. He was pretty incredible, if you know what I mean."

"Uh, yeah."

"I'm talkin' about in the sack."

"I got that."

"Nothin' like my husband."

"I get it."

The woman tried to touch his hand again, and Brody pulled back.

She ran her hand along the counter. "You own this place?"

"Yes."

Her eyes settled back on him. "I might just have to take up readin'."

"I know the feeling."

"Maybe we can be readin' buddies?" the woman suggested.

Brody searched for the teenager. Not seeing her, he hoped Travis would knock something off a shelf so he would have to pick it up. Finally, he looked back at the woman and asked, "You new in town?"

"Kinda," she said. "We came up to visit her fathah. We're only here for the night, then back home. But since we found this place," the woman leered at Brody, "we're gonna have to come to this sleepy berg some more."

"Where's home?"

"Boston."

"And your husband, he's up here?"

She nodded.

"What's he do?"

The woman's smile faded, and her eyes hardened. "Why you wanna know?"

"I don't," Brody said. "I was just making talk."

Her face twisted in anger. "You with the Feds?"

The big man's heart jumped. "What?"

"You a cop?"

He began to relax as he understood her old man must be in trouble with the law. He'd seen it before with guys in the crew. Their old ladies were as protective of them as mama bears were with their cubs.

"If you don't want to tell me who your husband is, keep it to yourself. I'm not interested in him."

Her eyes softened, and she reached for the back of his hand again. "Ya smooth talkah."

What happened? he wondered. He hadn't tried to encourage her interest in him.

"You were definitely a SEAL. I can tell."

"I never said that."

"You didn't have to." She giggled. "I can read between the lines. My husband is Frankie Columbo. Evah hear of him?"

Brody shook his head.

"He's sorta a big deal in these parts."

"Big deal, how?"

Her smile faded, and her eyes hardened.

Brody lifted his hands in mock surrender. "Like I said, just making conversation. Keep it to yourself."

She smiled again, happy with her small victory. "He owns all sorts of restaurants from Boston up to here."

Brody suddenly realized who the woman might be talking about it. "Which restaurant does he own in town?"

"The little joint around the corner. Makes the best meatball sandwiches."

"Il Cuoco Irato?"

"You mangled the way you say it, but yeah, that's the one."

Brody fell silent as he thought about what the woman said. She turned and looked for her stepdaughter. Not seeing the girl, she turned back to Brody.

"Ya know, I thought this was a fishing supply store before we walked in."

Brody's brow furrowed. "Why would you think that?"

"The Red Herring. Sort of a stupid name for a bookstore. Should be a bait and tackle shop."

Brody shrugged. "I didn't name it. I just bought it."

The teenager appeared then with Travis in one arm and put a paperback on the counter. It was *Pretty Little Liars* by Sara Shepard.

"This is a mystery?" Brody asked.

"Duh," the girl said, drawing out the word as if he should have known the answer to his question.

"What's it about?"

She frowned before answering. "Teenage girls up to no good."

The woman rolled her eyes and shook her head.

Unsure what to make of the girl, Brody flipped the book over and announced the price. "Twelve bucks."

"Ain't there sales tax?" the woman asked.

"Yeah," he said slowly. He hadn't paid attention to calculating the tax on the register when Onderdonk's people taught him the process during their two-day cram session to get him ready for life in the Witness Protection Program. "Don't worry about it. I'll cover it."

The woman reached into her wallet and pulled out a credit card. When she handed it to Brody, he stared at it. The name on the card read *Donna Columbo*. Processing a credit card was yet another thing he hadn't learned. The marshals gave so much information to him before arriving that it was like drinking from a firehose. He figured he would learn it sooner or later, but today was not going to be that day.

He handed the card back to Donna, who looked at him quizzically.

Brody then gave the book to the girl. "For you," he said. "Welcome to Pleasant Valley. You can keep the cat, too."

The teenager's demeanor softened. She then looked at the woman who disapprovingly shook her head.

"Not a chance, Chloe. Your fathah would kill me if you brought that mangy thing home."

The girl set Travis on the counter. "Thanks for the book, mister."

"You can call me Brody."

Chloe smiled and lifted the book in appreciation.

Donna guided the teenager toward the door, then turned back to the big man. "I'm coming back, Brody. I think I finally found a reason to be a readah."

"Thanks for the warning," he said.

She found his response charming and giggled on the way out the door.

Chapter 13

A couple more patrons came in during the afternoon. The first was a husband and wife visiting from North Bend, Oregon, as they made a loop through Maine. The husband, a roly-poly man with a genial smile, engaged Brody in conversation while his wife searched for a book. His forehead glistened from sweat and his T-shirt carried the logo for the U.S. Lighthouse Association.

Brody made the mistake of asking the man about the organization. He responded with a ten-minute explanation on the historical importance of lighthouses, their architectural beauty, and how he got involved with the association. Besides the tower in Pleasant Valley, Brody learned there were sixty-five more lighthouses scattered along the Maine coast, inlets, and islands, which earned it the nickname of The Lighthouse State.

The big man yawned as the husband continued to prattle. He didn't bother to cover his mouth, hoping the out-of-state man would read his boredom and stop talking. Unfortunately, the customer continued to chatter about lighthouses and the importance of maintaining a link to their storied pasts.

Brody looked for the wife, hoping she would have a question about a mystery book that he wouldn't be able to answer. She was nowhere to be seen, though, so he was stuck listening to the blathering husband.

The lighthouse lesson was so dull that Brody felt his eyes crossing. He wanted to yell at the man to shut up, to leave him alone, to walk into the ocean and become shark bait. The old Brody, Beau Smith, would have done just that. No, that's not true. The bookkeeper for the Satan's Dawgs would have physically removed this annoying Weeble from the store.

Except he couldn't do that now. That was against the marshal's rule of blending in. Therefore, he had to accept his current suffering. Brody Steele was a bookstore owner, and bookstore owners had to deal with these types. This was the penance the fates forced him to pay for being a rat, for turning against his crew. Brody had been to prison, and this continued tale of lighthouses was worse than that.

The cat walked out, saw the babbling rotund man, and made a hasty U-turn back into an aisle. Even Travis didn't want to hear the man.

Please, cat! Knock something over so I can pick it up.

But the tom was now suspiciously careful.

You traitor, Brody thought.

"So that's what brought us to Pleasant Valley," the husband said, wrapping up his long-winded monologue. "Now, after my wife picks a book, we'll move along to visit the various towns up and down the coast."

"There's a woman from Alabama doing the same thing."

The husband's face brightened. "She's touring all the lighthouses, too?"

"No," Brody said with a dismissive snort. "She's just traveling along the coast. She's got a day's head start on you though."

The husband blinked several times, not understanding what Brody was saying.

"If you hurry, you can catch her."

"Why would we want to do that?"

Brody shrugged. "Seems more fun than looking at stupid lighthouses."

The husband's jowls shook as he started to say something then stopped. Then he started and stopped again. Finally, he turned in a huff and stomped into an aisle. In a moment, he reappeared, leading his wife by the hand through the shop. She glanced at Brody with an apologetic look.

"Enjoy your lighthouse tour," Brody said to them.

The wife rolled her eyes before following her husband dutifully out of the store.

***

"So, it's true?"

"What's that?"

"You're claiming to be the new ownah of this here place."

Brody crossed his arms and studied the frail, older man. It was the same gentleman who sat next to him at the breakfast counter. He wore a short-sleeved yellow shirt, washed-out blue jeans, and gray running shoes. A faded Boston Red Sox hat sat cockeyed on his head.

"I am the new owner," Brody said.

"No, you're not. Alice Walkah would nevah have sold this place."

"Says who?"

"Says me. Herbert Paxton."

"Herbert?"

"It's a family name, wiseacre. People call me Herb."

"I'm Brody," he said, sticking his hand out.

Herb eyed it with disdain. "Don't go trying to make friends with me now, boy. I know you're up to something."

"I'm not up to anything."

"Alice Walkah is a decent woman. If you swindled her out of her business, I'll find out."

"I didn't swindle her out of anything."

"How much did you pay for this place?"

"That's none of your concern."

"Oh, it's my concern, boy," Herb said. "It most definitely *is* my concern."

Brody raised an eyebrow. "Was she your girlfriend?"

"No," Herb said defensively.

The big man smiled. "Ah."

"Don't 'ah' me like you know anything."

"I know enough to see that you liked her and are worried about her."

"You're darn right, I'm worried about her. You stand behind that counter like you own the place—"

"I *do* own the place."

"And you ain't told me where she is."

"You haven't asked."

Herb stopped talking then and glanced around, his brow crumpled as if in thought. Finally, he said, "You know where she is?"

"No."

"Well, why did you make me think you did?"

"I only said you didn't ask. Did she ever say anything about seeing a foreigner?"

"What do you mean 'see a foreignah'? This town gets tourists all year long. She was bound to see foreignahs."

"I meant, was she dating someone from another country?"

Herb shook his head in bewilderment. "What's your problem, boy?"

"I don't have one."

"Alice wasn't seeing anyone. She was heartbroken ovah the death of her sweetheart, Gilbert Griffiths."

"How long ago did he die?"

"I don't know," Herb said. "Maybe twenty years."

"Twenty years? People can get over something in that time."

The older man smirked. "You Navy boys are really something."

"Why does that make you mad?"

"Because she's a lady, and you talk about her like she's one of those girls who likes to go out with sailors." He bobbed his head, pleased with his verbal jabs.

Brody remained silent. Herb was clearly agitated about his insinuation that Alice was seeing someone.

"Tell me something," Herb said, "how did a squid like you supposedly buy this business?"

"I bought it on the Internet."

"The Internet?"

"It's a thing they do with computers now."

"I know what the Internet is, smart aleck. Just because you were a military man, doesn't mean I need to take any sass from you. I was in the Army, you know?"

Brody bowed apologetically.

Herbert studied him then. His voice softened, and he asked, "You really don't know where she is?"

"No, but I can ask the company that sold me the business if they know."

Herb nodded absently. "That would be good."

"So you and Alice were never boyfriend and girlfriend..."

The older man's eyes narrowed. "What is with you, boy?"

"I'm just trying to understand."

"She was a nice woman. You best remember that."

With that, Herb turned around and surveyed the bookstore for a moment. His shoulders dropped then, and his head slowly lowered before he shuffled toward the door.

Chapter 14

The elderly waiter seated them near the windows. "Here," he said and pulled out a chair for Daphne Winterbourne. When she began to sit, he pushed the chair underneath her.

Brody Steele sat with a view of the restaurant. Il Cuoco Irato was full that night. There must have been thirty people there. He hadn't seen any of these people in town the previous few days except for the three in the back corner. Those three he knew by name now—Frankie Columbo, his wife, Donna, and his daughter, Chloe.

The waiter handed Brody a menu and then gave one to Daphne. "Be back," he said in his clipped English and moved toward another table.

Daphne's eyes moved about the restaurant taking it all in. "This is so adorable. I can't believe we have a place this lovely in Pleasant Valley."

"Yeah," Brody said, his attention stuck on the corner booth.

"Have you ever been to Italy?"

"Hmm?"

"Italy?" Daphne said and pointed to the far wall where a mural of the country's map had been painted. "Ever been?"

"No," Brody said. "I haven't been outside of the United States unless you count Tijuana."

Daphne studied him. "But I thought you were... everyone is saying you were in the Navy."

Brody considered telling Daphne that the Navy had been a convenient lie, but he realized if he admitted to one truth, many more would have to follow. His whole story would unravel then. He'd lied plenty in his life, but he wished his new start in Pleasant Valley would allow him to be a different man and to have different relationships with people.

"You can't tell me, can you?" Daphne said, her voice low and conspiratorial.

"Excuse me?"

"You did something for the Navy that precludes you from telling me where you were. That's what it is." She tapped her lips as she thought. "What could it be?"

Brody grabbed his menu and opened it.

"The bookstore," she muttered.

His eyes lifted to hers.

"That's a clue, isn't it?"

"What?"

"You're smart. Smart guys in the military go into intelligence, right? You were military intelligence." Daphne studied him carefully and now tapped a fingernail against her teeth. "You were a naval spy, weren't you?"

Brody fought back a smile, but Daphne noticed it.

"Oh, my God! I knew it," she whispered. "You're like James Bond. He was a Commander in the Royal Navy. Did you know that?" He was about to protest, but she said, "Of course, you knew that. You own a mystery bookstore, duh? Sorry, I'm nervous."

"It's okay."

"Wait," she said, her brow creasing. "He was a spy after he got out of the navy, not while he was in. Isn't that right?"

Brody had no idea what she was talking about, having never read a Bond novel nor having watched one of the movies, but he responded as he thought she would want. "Sounds about right."

"I can't believe I guessed it. Well, you don't have to tell me anything more. I understand the duty of confidentiality binds you. That's what they make you swear to, right? Or do you have to sign?"

"Something like that."

Daphne smiled, then grabbed her menu. She opened her mouth in silent delight as she read each entry. Several times Daphne muttered, "Oh my," as her eyes danced over the possibilities. When she finished, she flipped it closed with satisfaction.

"Know what you're getting?" Brody asked.

"No," she said and started laughing. "There's so much to choose from. I can't decide."

"Why don't you pick one, it doesn't matter which, and I'll bring you back again so you can choose another. I'll keep bringing you back until you've had the entire menu."

"That sounds like a sneaky way to keep getting more dates."

"If you know about it beforehand, then it's not sneaky, is it?"

Daphne beamed. "Well then, I'm going to have a number three."

"What's a number three?"

"I have no idea," she said and giggled. "We'll find out."

The waiter walked up then. "Ready?" he asked.

After they finished their orders, he dutifully tucked their menus into the condiment holder and hurried back into the kitchen.

Brody noticed the teenager, Chloe, staring at him. When they made eye contact, she smiled. He nodded in return.

"Have you had any luck with the attorney?" Daphne asked.

"The attorney?"

"You were going to call the attorney and ask where Alice was living now."

"That's right," Brody said. "I'm sorry, I haven't done that yet. I will in the morning."

She tried to hide it, but her disappointment was palpable.

"I'll call him. I promise. I got sidetracked."

"I understand. You're still getting acquainted with the town, learning the ins and outs of the bookstore, meeting all sorts of new people. It must be overwhelming."

It wasn't said with sarcasm and snark. Daphne actually gave him the benefit of the doubt.

"Overwhelming, yes."

"And exciting?" she asked, her face brightening.

"Exciting?"

"I think owning a bookstore must be the most wonderful thing in the universe. To be surrounded by all those stories every day. It would be like... heaven."

Brody's eyes caught movement at the front door. The weightlifter he'd had the earlier confrontation with at his store walked in and proceeded directly toward the corner booth. He paused as he passed their table and eyed Brody, his lip curling in disgust, then he continued to Frankie Columbo's table.

"You know that guy?" Daphne asked.

"He came into my store."

"What kind of books does a guy like that read?"

"Children's books."

Daphne snorted then covered her face with a hand.

Brody smiled at her.

"I'm sorry," she said.

"Why?"

"I'm so embarrassed."

"You laughed. It's okay."

She shook her head.

"Hey," Brody said, "can I ask you a question about Constable Farnsworth?"

"Oh, no. *Emery*. What did he do?"

"What's the deal with him? He said you two were once..."

Daphne lowered her eyes for a moment. "Have you ever made a mistake you wish you could take back?"

Brody nodded. He had made a lifetime of bad choices he wished he could take back. Sitting across from this woman, in this town, made him especially regretful of past decisions.

"Emery is that mistake for me."

"What was wrong with him?"

"Beyond the constable thing?"

"Speaking of which, how did that begin?"

"We started watching some BBC mysteries, and he loved hearing how everyone called the local policeman a constable. He soon began telling people he was one."

"How did the chief of police take it?"

"There are only two people in the police department—"

"I heard that."

"So calling himself constable wasn't that big of a deal. It's sort of hard to find good help around here."

"Okay, so how did you two start? He doesn't seem to be in your league."

Her cheeks flushed, and she looked away. "That's funny. Everyone was telling me that I was lucky to go out with Emery. That he was kind and sweet. That he's handsome."

"He's not *that* handsome," Brody quickly interjected.

"I found him to be completely boring."

"I can see that."

"He always wanted to go bike riding. Sometimes for hours on end. Ugh. No, thanks."

Brody was leaned in and concentrating on Daphne, so he missed her approaching.

"Excuse me."

The teenager stood next to him. She still wore black jeans and her black Vans, but she now wore a turquoise blouse that softened her overall appearance. Her thick black mascara had been removed as well.

"Hi, Chloe." Brody turned to his date. "Daphne, this is Chloe."

The two women shook hands.

"Chloe came by my store today."

"I wanted to say thanks for the book. I'm about halfway through it."

Brody's face registered his surprise. "Already?"

Chloe shrugged. "It's an easy book."

"Not for me," Brody said.

The teenager chuckled.

"What book are you reading?" Daphne asked.

"*Pretty Little Liars*. It's by Sara Shepard."

"Oh, I've read it," Daphne said. "Don't you love it?"

"So far, it's great."

As the two women spoke, Brody's attention drifted to the back booth. The weightlifter was whispering into the ear of Frankie Columbo, whose eyes remained on Brody. For a moment, he held onto Columbo's gaze, not breaking away. When he finally did, he caught Donna Columbo staring intently at him. When they made eye contact, she winked slowly, then licked her upper lip.

Brody looked back to the women at his table. Daphne held Chloe's hand. "You should read it next," Daphne said. "You'll love it."

To Brody, Chloe asked, "Do you have it?"

"Have what?"

"*The Talented Mr. Ripley*," the teenager said.

"Ripley?"

Daphne laughed and touched his hand. "Oh, he has it. I've seen it there many times. Trust me. You'll love it."

"I better get back," Chloe said. "I just wanted to say hi and thanks. It was nice to meet you, Daphne."

As they watched the teenager return to her table, Daphne said, "She seems like a sweet girl."

"Travis seemed to like her."

The weightlifter climbed out of the booth, allowing Chloe to get in and slide over to her father. Frankie didn't even acknowledge his daughter as she moved closer. The teenager sat dutifully next to him, though, her look calm and disinterested.

As the weightlifter walked by on his way out of the restaurant, he averted his gaze even though Brody tried to make eye contact. The man wasn't paying attention and bumped into the old waiter, knocking a tray of dirty dishes from his hands to the floor, the noise resonating through the small restaurant.

The waiter's face flushed, he threw his hands in the air and spoke in hurried Italian. The weightlifter dismissively waved off the older man then glared at Brody for a moment. He then hurried out of the restaurant.

"What was that about?" Daphne asked.

"I don't know. Maybe he was late for a pump."

***

After dinner, Brody walked Daphne home. She lived nearby in the 500 block of Red Street. As they strolled, she continued to talk about dinner.

"That risotto was heavenly, wasn't it?"

"I only had one bite." She'd let him have a taste of her rice dish.

"But don't you think it was to die for?"

Brody shook his head. "No food is worth dying for."

She fell silent for a moment then said, "I hadn't thought of it like that."

He grunted a non-committal response. They had already talked for almost three hours. That was the most talking he'd done ever. *In his life.* He must like this girl if he was willing to engage in conversation for that long, but even that had its limits.

"Unless you're starving," Daphne said.

"Huh?"

"Food is worth dying for if you're starving. You'd fight for it if you were hungry, wouldn't you?"

Brody didn't answer as words now escaped him. Even though it was almost ten o'clock, he wasn't tired. Quite the opposite. He had enjoyed the evening with the beautiful Daphne Winterbourne, but he just wasn't a man built for long conversations. It was time to end the night.

"Here's my house," she announced.

They stood under a streetlight, so he had trouble making out the color of the house. However, he could see the white picket fence and the brightly colored flowers that peaked through the slats.

"I had a lovely time," Daphne said.

"Me, too."

"I hope we can do it again."

"We will."

She stood on her tiptoes, and he bent down, closing his eyes. He opened them after she kissed him on the side of the cheek.

He watched as she ran up the sidewalk to her house. When she disappeared inside, he thought to himself that Daphne was nothing like the girls who used to hang out with the motorcycle club. With those girls, he would have skipped the dinner date and taken them straight to bed.

However, tonight felt more fulfilling even if he was mentally spent from all the talking.

When the front porch light clicked off, he headed home.

Chapter 15

The air was humid, and the moon was almost full. A horn from a boat signaled in the distance.

Thoughts of his date were still in his head when Brody thought he heard the shuffling of feet. He spun around, but no one was there. He remained still for a moment, listening.

I'm hearing things, he thought.

He soon dismissed his concerns and continued home. As he walked, he listened for small noises, but he didn't pick them out any further. Instead, he heard a boat horn again. This time it sounded like it came from elsewhere in the ocean.

Nearing the bookstore, he knew he wasn't yet ready for bed, so he kept walking and headed toward the shore. The more he walked, the better he felt. He'd gotten over the earlier suspicion that someone was following him, and now his thoughts floated back to Daphne, the town, and his new life.

By being sent to this community, he had an opportunity to reinvent himself, to become a better man. He hadn't initially intended to have those thoughts, but they sort of snuck up on him. Brody wasn't going to ignore them, though. He was going to embrace them and see where they led.

The lighthouse stood proudly on the edge of the beach, illuminating the shore. Brody noticed a dark form on the water and squinted. It appeared to be a small boat motoring slowly away from the Pleasant Valley beach.

Across the channel were New Hampshire and another lighthouse. Was the boat heading in that direction?

When the boat disappeared into the darkness, Brody watched the lighthouse in the distance. Its light rotated gently in circles until it suddenly stopped and focused on one area of the channel. Was the lighthouse guiding the little boat safely to the harbor?

If so, what was it carrying?

And why couldn't they just drive it up Interstate 95?

Sneaking anything across the channel didn't make sense.

A horn sounded in the far distance.

Brody turned to leave the beach, and a shadowy figure sprinted up Main Street.

Someone *had* been watching him.

He instinctively crouched, his senses now on high alert. As he began the trek back to his apartment, every corner presented a new danger, and every storefront was an opportunity for someone to lunge out. Brody wished he had a gun or, at least, a knife. Even as Brody Steele, he wasn't allowed to own a firearm. U.S. Marshal's rules. But a knife, *that* he could own.

Earlier, he perspired due to the night's humidity. Now, he was sweating profusely due to intense concentration. Each time he moved, he remained in a crouch, moving purposively from door to door, his eyes scanning the quiet streets. When he made it to his block, he strode into the alley and stopped.

Walking up the steps to his apartment was a fatal funnel. If someone was atop them, they could shoot down, and he'd have nowhere to go. Or the reverse was true as well, if he was ascending them, they could attack him from the bottom of the stairs, and he'd have nowhere to flee.

Brody wasn't going to allow himself to be scared though. Caution was one thing; scared was out of the question. Sensing the area was clear, he hurried to the steps, and took them two at a time until he was in front of his apartment door. It only took him seconds to step inside.

When he relocked the door, he finally relaxed. A nagging thought finally made its way to the forefront of his mind.

What was *really* going on in Pleasant Valley?

Chapter 16

It was a fitful night of rest. For a long time, he felt on the verge of sleep, his mind drifting from thoughts of the Satan's Dawgs to Daphne Winterbourne to Frankie Columbo and back again.

He wasn't apprehensive about Columbo. It was something else. It was the understanding that the man didn't belong in Pleasant Valley any more than he did. Brody knew his purpose for being in this idyllic town but didn't understand why Columbo chose to be there.

What did Pleasant Valley provide him?

It was apparent why he thought about Daphne. She was pretty and smart, the type of woman who would never have paid attention to Beau Smith, bookkeeper for the Satan's Dawgs. Throughout the night, he wondered how she would react to the news he had been a member of an outlaw motorcycle club, that he had been one of their leaders and had killed men who crossed them.

Then he thought about the Phoenix-based club. They were part of a tight knit, but loosely affiliated network of motorcycle clubs across the nation. Word spread through them like wildfire when it concerned rats. He wouldn't be able to safely go anywhere in the country where there were motorcycle clubs. His life would forever be spent looking over his shoulder.

When he finally fell asleep, it was with the thought of himself as a traitor to the Dawgs. It had been something he'd fallen asleep to for more than a year now.

***

After a shower, he dressed and made a cup of coffee. He walked down from his apartment into the rear of the bookstore. He didn't bother to turn on the lights and wandered straight to the sales counter. He powered on the computer, sipping his coffee while it came to life.

On the edge of the monitor hung several items—a username and password to AbeBooks, a yellow sticky note with Carrie Fenton's name and phone number, and a tattered business card for Manchester Mechanical and Heating.

Something fell to the floor. Brody thought about yelling at the cat but figured it would accomplish nothing this morning. It hadn't changed the mangy tom's behavior so far. He sipped his coffee, and the cat sauntered into the middle of the store. They eyed each other for a moment.

"Who's feeding you?" Brody asked.

Travis didn't bother responding.

"You know I'm not going to do that, right?"

The cat lifted a paw and dragged his tongue across it.

"Cough up a furball, and that will be the last one you do."

Travis paused and eyed him as if he was considering his words. A crooked smile played at the edges of Brody's lips. Maybe they were reaching an understanding. Then the cat returned to cleaning himself.

Brody grunted and focused on the computer. He set his coffee cup down then started the Internet browser. Google appeared on the monitor. With two fingers, he slowly entered "Frankie Columbo mob."

The screen filled with a list of entries. Brody selected the third story down with the headline *Frankie the Dove Cleared in Money Laundering Scheme.* According to *The Boston Herald*, Francis Columbo was an underboss with the Rosa crime family. He'd been arrested and charged with money laundering. Various names were connected to the story, none of which he had ever heard, except for the mention of his wife, Donna. The article was written about a year prior.

He clicked a couple of other articles, but they said the same thing.

Francis 'Frankie the Dove' Columbo was a mobster who specialized in money laundering. There was no explanation as to why he was called 'the Dove.'

Brody considered Pleasant Valley then. For laundering illegally gotten gains, the Dove would need a variety of businesses that would appear legitimate. The more cash-based, the better. The mob funnels dirty money into a front, and real taxable profits come out. A little restaurant in a tourist town might fit the bill nicely.

Donna Columbo stated her husband owned restaurants from Boston up to this little town. Maybe Frankie the Dove's presence in Pleasant Valley wasn't so abnormal after all.

A throaty roar ripped him from his thoughts, and he looked up to the window. Another roar tore through the morning's silence. A rider on a Harley Davidson slowly passed by the window of the bookstore.

Brody jumped from his stool, raced around the counter, and hid behind a bookshelf as he peered through the window.

The rider stopped on the other side of the store to let a young couple safely cross the street. He wore a shiny black half-helmet that showed his clean-cut hairstyle. His leather jacket bore a back patch that read *Ride Free* on the top rocker and *Maine, USA* across the bottom. The rider smiled and waved at the couple as they passed in front of his bike.

Brody relaxed and slowly let out the breath he hadn't realized he was holding.

It was only a wannabe, probably some corporate type with 2.5 kids at home, pretending to be an outlaw on his $20,000 motorcycle.

Born to be mild, he mused.

He turned from the window and smiled. The grin faded when he felt his heart still pounding inside his chest. He lifted his hands to discover them shaking.

Brody stood in the silence of his bookstore.

Is this who I've become now? he wondered. *The once-feared bookkeeper now frightened by the sight of a corporate hack on a Harley Fat Boy?*

A frown creased his face.

Chapter 17

When his stomach rumbled, Brody cleaned himself up and headed to A Pleasant Meal. The little restaurant was full again, and the only seat available was at the counter next to Herb Paxton.

After he slipped onto the chair, the older man turned to him. When recognition clicked in, Herb's smile slowly faded.

"Good morning," Brody said.

"Morning," Herb mumbled as he turned his attention back to his cup of black coffee.

The waitress in the brown apron appeared. "The usual?" she asked.

He'd only been in once, so he was surprised if she could recall it after a single visit. "If you can remember it," Brody said, "then yes."

"Black coffee. Three scrambled eggs. Hash browns. Sausage links, not patties." Her eyes rolled up and to the left as she thought. When she latched onto something, she returned her gaze to Brody. "And a banana to go."

He nodded his approval.

She completed an order receipt and hung it on the ticket wheel for the short-order cooks. She filled a mug of coffee and placed it in front of Brody. Then she veered off into the restaurant to help another customer.

Brody turned to Herb. "Can I ask you something?"

The older man lifted his head but didn't bother to face Brody. "You find out where Alice is?"

"Not yet."

"Then no," Herb said, "you cannot ask me a question." He lifted his cup of coffee and took a sip.

"It's about Alice."

The older man eyed Brody.

"What can you tell me about her? Have you known her the entire time she was here?"

Herb lowered his cup and stared into the coffee for so long Brody thought the man was ignoring him. Finally, he said, "She changed a lot over the years."

"How so?"

"When she first got here, she was young. In her twenties. She was man-crazy at the time."

The way Herb said it revealed he didn't approve of that time in Alice Walker's life.

"It was the early eighties, and times were different, I guess. She had some suitors from as far away as York Harbah and Eliot. When a woman's got man-fevah, guys are attracted to her like moths to a porch light."

Brody sipped his coffee and watched Herb struggle with his words.

"You know how these stories go. She eventually fell in love with a man. Gilbert Griffiths. Ol' Gil was nice enough, I suppose. Nicah than most of the ones she ran around with at the time. He lived ovah in Rollinsford.

They carried on a relationship for almost twenty years."

Herb fell silent as he watched the short-order cooks.

"They never married?"

He shook his head. "Nevah. They didn't even live together."

"For twenty years?"

"Thereabouts, yeah. Rumor had it Alice was the one who refused to get hitched."

"Why?"

Herb shrugged. "She nevah explained herself on anything to anyone. She ain't that kind of woman."

"And Gil was okay with it?"

"If he wasn't, he nevah said nothing about it. The two of them did things togethah every day. Most folks considered them married, even though they lived twenty minutes apart."

"That's probably why they stayed together for so long," the big man said.

Herb fell silent again, and Brody left him to his thoughts. It was evident the older man cared for Alice, but the affection had only been one way.

After a few minutes, Herb said, "When Gil got sick, Alice took care of him. She was special that way. His death tore her up. It was sad to see the change in her. She wasn't the same."

"You're sweet on her."

"Hard not to be. Alice Walkah is a real beauty." He sipped his coffee.

"Notice anything lately about her? Maybe a change in how she acted or her habits?"

The older man thought about it for a moment. "The only real change I noticed was when she started hanging out with that youngah woman. About a year ago. They met through the bookstore."

"What were they doing?"

"Alice told me that the woman was a writah. She'd originally come into the store for some books to read. The two of them started talking about stories, and suddenly Alice was helping her develop some ideas for a new mystery."

"Really? Did you meet her?"

"A couple times. She's kind of an intense lady."

"Intense, how?"

He gnawed on his lower lip while he thought. "She's got those eyes that take everything in. Like a hawk."

Or a cop.

"Remember her name?" Brody asked.

"Carrie something or other. Her books have their own display at the front of the store. It shouldn't be hard to find." Herb's eyes drifted suspiciously to Brody. "Especially for the new ownah of The Red Herring."

Carrie Fenton, Brody thought. Her books were on display at the front of the store. He'd also seen a little sticky note stuck to the computer that had her phone number written on it.

"What else can you tell me about her? Carrie Fenton, I mean."

Herb seemed disappointed that Brody ignored his slight. He stared back into his coffee. "I guess she's nice. About my granddaughter's age. Too many tattoos for my taste."

"How many is too many?"

"On a girl? One."

Brody smiled. The older man wouldn't have liked any of the girls that hung around the motorcycle club.

"Whenevah I came around, Alice and Carrie would stop talking. It always seemed like they were scheming up something."

"Scheming?"

"Yeah," Herb said. "You know how two women can be together, sharing secrets and laughs. It was like they were always making plans for something."

"Does Carrie live in town?"

"No. She lives over in the big city."

"Boston?"

"Dover."

Chapter 18

The brass bell chimed loudly just before the door banged against the far wall. The cat, who had been sitting calmly in the middle of the shop, bolted down the aisle labeled Noir, sending several books to the floor.

The weightlifter stomped into the store and pointed his finger at Brody. "Why were you down at the lighthouse?"

Brody calmly put down *The Deep Blue Goodby*. "You were following me?"

The bell rang again as the bookstore's door finally closed.

"I'm gonna ask ya again nicely—"

"The first time was nice?"

"Why were ya at the lighthouse last night?"

"I was taking a walk."

The weightlifter repeatedly poked his finger in the air, accenting his words. "You're stickin' ya beak in where it don't belong."

Brody stepped from around the counter. "What are you going to do about it?"

The weightlifter eyed Brody. "I don't want to fight no veteran."

"Lucky for me, I'm not one," he said.

The weightlifter's eyes widened, "What?"

"I lied."

"Ya lied about bein' a veteran? That's unpatriotic."

Brody shrugged.

"I should punch your teeth in for that."

"You could try."

The weightlifter slowly shook his head as he made up his mind. Finally, his head stopped moving, but he continued to think. Suddenly, he reared back as he readied a punch.

The bigger man didn't hesitate, though, and punched the store's visitor.

"Hey!" the weightlifter cried and covered his injured eye with his left hand. He then swung wildly with his right.

Brody ducked the punch and hit his opponent in the stomach.

This doubled-over the weightlifter. Brody took his time setting his feet before he socked the interloper in his uncovered eye.

When the weightlifter hit the ground, it was with a heavy thump. He lay unconscious on the large area rug.

Brody stood there and played back the moment. He wasn't a man built for regret, but he immediately understood there might have been a better way for him to have handled that moment. However, Brody was in the thick of it now. He had hit the hornet's nest, so there was only one thing to do now.

Hit it again.

Brody grabbed the edges of the rug and dragged the unconscious weightlifter out onto the sidewalk. The man was heavier than he imagined, and it took some extra effort to pull him over the store's threshold.

When they were outside, the morning's humidity quickly clung to him, and the ocean's aroma tickled his nose. Brody stood and put his hands on his hips, trying to catch his breath. Several passersby stopped to watch.

"Everything okay?" an old man asked.

Brody nodded. "He insulted the Navy."

The older man shook his head. "When will they learn?" He walked off without further concern.

It took several yanks to roll the weightlifter off the rug and into the street. Brody didn't want him on the sidewalk, blocking access to The Red Herring.

He carried the carpet back into his store, repositioned it, and returned to his book.

***

He had only made it through a couple of pages when the cops arrived, their lights and sirens blaring. That might be a bit of an exaggeration. Constable Emery Farnsworth showed up with a siren wailing on the handlebars of his bicycle. He skidded to a stop, the back of his bike sliding proudly out.

Brody watched the noisy arrival of the officer through the window with mild fascination. It was like watching a kid showing off to his parents.

After silencing the siren, the constable swung his leg over the bike seat and dropped the kickstand. He patted the bicycle once before surveying the scene.

The weightlifter was seated on the curb, rubbing his head. Farnsworth unbuckled his helmet and pushed it back on his head, like an old west sheriff. The two men spoke for several minutes before Brody lost interest and returned to his book.

In the rear of the store, something thudded. Brody didn't bother yelling at the cat though. He didn't have the enthusiasm for it, and it still wouldn't make a difference. The cat didn't listen to him. Maybe he needed to call him something other than Travis. It was clear from his reading of *The Deep Blue Good-by* that Travis McGee rarely followed the rules. He'd chosen an unfortunate name for the cat.

He finished another page before the bell rang, interrupting a McGee monologue. Brody was starting to enjoy the inner thoughts of the Florida detective.

"What happened out there?" the constable asked.

"Out where?"

"There," Farnsworth said, pointing to where the weightlifter still sat.

"I don't know. What happened?" Brody asked.

Farnsworth exhaled loudly, and he disapprovingly shook his head. "You know what happened, Brody. There's a young man out there who looks like he got hit by a freight train."

"Oh, him."

"Yes, him."

"We disagreed about my return policy."

"He said it was because you lied about being a Navy veteran."

Brody shook his head. "I wouldn't do that."

"So, you are a veteran?"

"Definitely." With all the lying about his veteran status, Brody figured he would have to talk to Onderdonk about somehow getting that added to his cover.

Outside the store, the weightlifter shakily stood and looked through the window at Brody and Emery.

"Were there any witnesses to the altercation?"

"Besides the cat?" Brody said.

Farnsworth glanced around. "Where is Magnum, by the way? The little guy used to love me."

"He's rearranging the *Thriller* section."

"He's doing what?" Farnsworth asked, taking a step toward the book aisles.

Brody cleared his throat. "What are you going to do about the fight, Emery? It was just him and me inside the store with no witnesses. The best you've got is mutual combat."

The constable turned and eyed him suspiciously. "Been in some fights as a bookseller?"

"This was my first time as a bookstore owner, but as a sailor, I've been in a few."

"Let's not make it a habit, Brody. Pleasant Valley isn't known for this kind of behavior."

The weightlifter began walking away with his shoulders rolled forward. Emery caught the movement and watched the man. "He said he wouldn't press charges if you won't."

"Sounds fair to me."

Both the officer and the bookseller watched as the dejected man disappeared around the corner.

"Want me to tell him he's trespassed?" Emery asked. "That way, he won't be able to come around your store again."

"With his type," Brody said, "it wouldn't make a difference."

Chapter 19

"What's with you and the bicycle cop?"

Brody spun around to find U.S. Marshal Ted Onderdonk standing in the middle of the bookstore. He wore a short-sleeve plaid shirt, khaki Dockers, and a pair of brown loafers. The bell had not sounded when he entered.

"How'd you do that?"

"What?"

"Get in here without setting off the bell."

"It's a marshal secret."

"Ekleberry knew how to do it, too."

"Max was here?"

Brody nodded.

"What did he want?"

"To check on me."

Onderdonk's eyes swept the bookstore. "Huh."

"Yeah. Huh."

"So, why was the rent-a-cop here? He looked serious."

"I had a fight."

The lawman returned his focus to Brody. "A fight? You're supposed to keep a low profile."

"It's hard when the mob's in town."

Onderdonk's eyes slanted. "The mob is here? Where?"

"Couple blocks down. Little Italian joint. It's a front."

The marshal moved to the window and pointed. "Down that way?"

"Uh-huh."

Onderdonk was quiet as he watched the foot traffic on Main Street.

"You going to tell me what happened to Alice Walker?" Brody asked.

The lawman turned slowly to face him. "Alice?"

"Don't play dumb."

Onderdonk remained silent as he studied the big man.

"You told me there was a recent opening in one of the businesses the Marshal Service owned. Remember that?"

"I remember."

"But there wasn't any opening, was there? It wasn't like someone quit or retired. Alice went missing. She's been so for several weeks."

Something fell in the back of the store, but Brody ignored it. Onderdonk tilted his head as he listened for further noise.

"Maybe you knew this, maybe you didn't, but the town folks liked Alice. A lot. They also liked this store. When you plugged me in here, did you know they'd come checking on her?"

The lawman's face relaxed.

"The town is suspicious of me, Ted. A couple of them wonder if I had something to do with her disappearance."

"That's ridiculous."

"How would they know otherwise?"

"You weren't even around when she disappeared."

Brody rubbed his naked chin. "Someone saw her talking with you in Manchester a couple of days before she went missing."

"How do they know it was me?"

"They don't, but I do. The woman said the man was dressed like me."

Onderdonk's eyes took in Brody's plaid shirt, his khaki pants, and his loafers. "You are a snappy dresser."

"I look like you, Ted."

"There's a lot of guys dressed like this."

"But only one U.S. Marshal handling a witness in Pleasant Valley. You didn't pull her out of her cover, did you?"

Onderdonk took a deep breath, then puffed his cheeks as he blew it out. "No, I did not pull her out."

"Where is she?"

"I don't know."

"So, she is missing?"

The lawman nodded, then stepped over to the book spinner and turned it.

"The computer mix-up. You checking into it. All of it was a lie."

Onderdonk pulled a copy of James Ziskin's *Cast the First Stone* from the spinner and flipped it over to the back. "Ever read this?"

"Don't ignore me."

The marshal carefully tucked the book back into its resting place. "It was a ruse."

"A ruse? You're using me as bait, trying to figure out what happened to her."

"That was my plan."

Brody's face warmed, and he moved near the lawman. "You planned to make me a worm on a hook."

Onderdonk rolled his eyes. "Now relax, Beau."

"Beau? Beau! You and Ekleberry killed Beau! There's only Brody now."

He grabbed the marshal by the shirt, jerking him closer. Onderdonk's eyes widened briefly, but he didn't lift his hands to protect himself.

Brody's heart rate pounded in his ears. "Better fight back."

"When you lost your temper," the marshal said, "I already won."

"Last chance." His anger was at full boil. He wanted to hurt the lawman, to take a piece of retribution. "You either fight back, or I'm going to tear your head off."

"You won't touch me," the marshal said, his voice eerily calm.

Brody had had enough of the lawman's arrogance, but before he could throw a strike, Onderdonk grabbed his hand, which still held the marshal's shirt. With a quick twist, the lawman stepped backward and flipped the big man to the ground.

The resulting thud brought Travis scrambling from the rear of the store to see what the commotion was. The two men remained in that frozen position—Brody on his back, Onderdonk holding him by the wrist.

"You okay?" the lawman asked.

"No," Brody rasped.

Onderdonk sighed. "Anything broke?"

"I don't think so."

He released Brody's hand and stepped away. When the big man stood, he brushed himself off, more out of habit than for any dirt he'd collected from the floor of the bookstore. He realized he was doing the same thing Ekleberry had done after his hat was knocked off.

"Hey kitty," Onderdonk said as Travis rubbed against his leg.

"You know Alice but don't know the rule about the cat?"

The marshal looked up as he petted the tom. "The name rule? Of course, I do. But I read science fiction, and the rule was for mystery protagonists. Alice was very clear about that. When I tried to name him Deckard, she got all up in arms. She refused to hear my argument that *Do Androids Dream of Electric Sheep?* was science fiction crime noir."

Brody shook his head. "This place," he muttered and ambled behind the counter while rubbing his wrist.

The marshal followed him. "I hope you fought the other guy better than you fought me."

"I did."

"What was the donnybrook about?"

"He's muscle for the mob front I told you about. He didn't like that I was down near the lighthouse last night."

Onderdonk's eyes slanted. "Something going on down there?"

"I don't know. It was a nice night, and there aren't many other things to do here."

The lawman picked up the knitting needles and yarn from the counter. "I see what you mean."

"Don't make fun," he said. "It keeps my mind off my predicament."

"Who taught you how to do this?"

"My grandmother."

"The same one who Ekleberry...?"

Brody nodded. "The same."

Onderdonk tossed the knitting kit onto the counter. "So, the mob is in Pleasant Valley?"

"You didn't know?"

"No."

"And Alice didn't tell you?"

"Nope."

"Would you have left her here if you knew they were only a few blocks away?"

"Not a chance."

"Okay, Ted. I think it's time you tell me about Alice," Brody said, taking a seat on the stool.

Chapter 20

"In nineteen seventy-eight, she was a cocktail waitress in Chicago. She was Evelyn Spier then. Evie to her friends." Onderdonk leaned on the counter.

Brody crossed his arms. "Evelyn Spier. Chicago. Got it."

"I learned most of this from reviewing her file. When all this went down, I was still a punk kid. I talked to Alice a little about what happened, but she got defensive about it, a little elusive, and she painted herself as the victim."

He lifted his chin and raised his eyebrows, an indication for Onderdonk to continue with his story.

"All right, Beau. Just relax. I don't get to tell a story very often, and you're already rushing me. Takes all the enjoyment right out of it."

"You're killing me, Ted."

Onderdonk smiled. "So, in seventy-eight, Evie was twenty-years-old and a real pretty thing."

"How do you know? She's old enough to be your mother."

"I saw her picture in the file; that's how. Back then, the drinking age for beer and wine was nineteen. Hard alcohol was twenty-one. The club where she worked let her serve it all. Now, where she was employed doesn't matter, but what does is who took a shine to her. His name was Daniel O'Leary. Danny Boy to his friends. Officer O'Leary to everyone else."

The big man clucked his tongue against the roof of his mouth. "A cop."

"A dirty cop."

Brody's eyebrows rose. "Ah, a useful one."

Onderdonk rolled his eyes. "He was dirty in the wrong way."

"There's a right way?"

"When you're in the hip pocket of the local don, it's the wrong way. Too many things are going to come back to haunt you."

Some books fell to the floor in the back of the store, and Onderdonk glanced toward the noise.

"The cat," Brody said. "He doesn't like how the books are color-coordinated."

Onderdonk opened his mouth to say something then paused, considering what Brody said. He turned to look for the cat. Finally, the marshal continued. "The first time he ever saw her, Daniel O'Leary, thirty-one years-old, five foot ten, dark hair, and recently divorced, fell head over heels for the supposedly sweet and innocent Evie Spier."

"*Supposedly* sweet and innocent?"

"I'll get to that in a minute. I'm telling a story here."

Brody apologetically lifted his hands.

"The two of them began a hot and heavy courtship, and before long they moved in together. It was the seventies, remember, and people did that sort of thing. Unfortunately for

Danny Boy, nobody ever told him that he had a bad habit of talking in his sleep."

Brody grimaced. "Not good."

"You're paying attention. So one night, Danny mumbled a guy's name. For whatever reason, Evie was awake, and she heard it. She didn't think anything of it. Until a couple of days later, the guy was gunned down in an alley. Evie read about it in the *Tribune*. It seems the police suspected it was a mob hit.

"If she were a different kind of girl, maybe Evie would have thought her cop boyfriend was a psychic or something, but Evie knew the score, including what a cop's salary looked like. She realized Danny couldn't afford to take her out as often as they went or to buy her nice dresses on that alone. Early on, she knew he was on the take, and she was okay with it. She wanted the better things in life, and, the way she figured it, you had to get a little dirty to get those things."

"Smart girl."

Onderdonk ignored Brody's comment. "So, Evie started sleeping a little lighter. She wanted to hear what Danny was going to let slip next in his sleep. A couple of nights later, she heard it. He mumbled something about a gambling joint down on the waterfront. In the morning, she checked the Tribune—nothing. The next day— nothing. On the third day, though, a suspected underground casino burned to the ground. The newspaper reported it as the fallout from a mob war brewing on the streets of Chicago."

"It was probably a joint that wouldn't get under the mob's protection."

"The investigating detectives had those same thoughts."

Brody pursed his lips and squinted as he listened. He was enjoying Onderdonk's tale of Evelyn Spier.

"Now," the marshal said, "Evie Spier had big aspirations for a twenty-year-old. She didn't want to be a cocktail waitress her whole life. She wanted to go someplace. As they used to say in those days, she was a smart broad."

"Say it now, and you're likely to get punched in the mouth."

"I wouldn't dare," Onderdonk said. "Anyway, Evie figured there was an angle in it for her, so she got a couple of meatheads together."

"She had guys?"

"Do you know any pretty girl that can't pull some dunderheads to help her?"

"Good point," Brody said with a half-hearted shrug. "But why didn't she tell good ol' Danny Boy he was talking in his sleep? You said she knew he was dirty, and that she was okay with it."

Onderdonk stared at him like he was simple.

It took him a minute to figure it out. Finally, Brody said, "Because she already knew he wasn't the one."

"As I said, she was a smart broad."

"Which you wouldn't say in polite company."

"Of course not. I've had the company's sexual harassment training. Anyway, Evie figured she'd make a couple of scores off his pillow talk, dump him, and then she'd be set to find a new prince charming."

"I see why you said she was *supposedly* sweet."

"She assembled her little crew and told them to stand by for a call. It didn't take long for Danny Boy to mumble his way into trouble. He mentioned another name, but this time it was a numbers house."

"Illegal betting?"

"Uh-huh, right. The place was disguised as a taxi company. Her crew knocked it over before her boyfriend and his buddies could do it. It worked like a charm, too, and she got a fat roll of cash out of it. She hid the money at her mother's house and began thinking about doing the next job. In her mind, how could the mob get upset if they were only lending a hand, right?"

"They were helpers is what they were."

Onderdonk chuckled. "Except when Officer Daniel O'Leary came home that night, he was more than a little agitated. He wouldn't tell Evie what was wrong. He kept it bottled up inside. It was temporary though. He soon got drunk, smacked her around, which was normal, by the way. I don't think I told you that."

"You didn't tell me that. That seems like an important detail in this story."

"Yeah, Danny would get drunk occasionally and take out his frustrations on Evie."

"Another reason why she would realize he wasn't the one."

"You would hope," the lawman said. "Anyway, when he woke up the next morning Danny Boy apologized for what he did—"

"Of course."

"—and he went back to work, protecting and serving the great city of Chicago. Evie returned to slinging drinks, presumably with heavy makeup to disguise a black eye. Everything was back to normal."

"Until the next time he mumbled in his sleep," Brody added.

"Now, you're playing along with the rhythm," Onderdonk said. "Except the next time Danny mumbled in his sleep, it was about killing a man. Evie was smart enough to ignore it. There was no money for her in that type of job. Her crew just wanted to knock over places the mob wanted robbed. She felt that was a safe scam."

"There's no safe scam with the mob."

"Prophetic words. Evie was sleeping light, listening for anything that could lead her to another score, when she finally heard something. The boyfriend mentioned a dry cleaner. It wasn't much to go on, but she knew it had to be another numbers joint.

"Evie was so excited she could hardly contain herself. In the morning, she called her boys. They found the dry cleaner Danny Boy mentioned and hit it fast, completely cleaning it out."

"Was it a betting parlor?" Brody asked.

Onderdonk nodded slowly. "It was, for sure. The haul was bigger than the first. Evie's cut was so big she figured she could grab the money from her mom's house and take off. Leave Daniel O'Leary and his drunken hands behind. Maybe go out to sunny California and start a new life."

Brody moved off the stool and put his hands on the counter. "By the look on your face, Ted, I see this is where her story goes bad."

"The numbers house they hit—"

"—was Danny Boy's employer. It was a mob joint, wasn't it?"

"Nothing was supposed to happen to it. When Danny Boy came home after the dry cleaner was robbed, it was a whole different kind of agitated. He didn't drink, he didn't talk, and he didn't even hit her. He was quiet and withdrawn. She asked what was wrong, and he told her it was the job and to leave him alone while he figured out his problem. She did, of course, and gave him a wide berth." Onderdonk drummed his fingers on the counter. "Evie knew exactly why Danny was angry. She didn't need a road map, but she wasn't freaking out. No one knew it was her crew. She figured they had been smart. They wore masks, and no one spoke more than they had to during the heist. Also, no one was supposed to spend the money they took either. Everything would be okay if they just played it all by the book."

Brody shook his head. "Only somebody didn't play it by the book." He'd been through this with some of his old crew—guys who couldn't keep their greed and selfishness in check.

Onderdonk's smile was crooked. "About a week went by, and Evie wasn't even trying to sleep light anymore. Now, she couldn't even nap when Danny Boy was around. She was afraid. She lay in bed and listened to him snore all night long. Then she heard him mutter a name, a name she knew well."

"Hers?"

Onderdonk shook his head. "One of her boys."

"Ah."

"The mob had discovered her boys were involved with the robbery and were siccing Danny Boy on him. Evie knew it would only be a matter of time until she was discovered. And if she was found out, she knew she was dead. Evie lay in bed that night thinking it through."

"She couldn't call the cops," Brody said.

"Right," the lawman agreed. "Her boyfriend was dirty, and since he wasn't doing the jobs by himself, maybe there were more dirty cops in the department."

"And if she went to the police," Brody said, "she would have to admit what she'd done."

"Exactly. If she went down to the local precinct, Evie was pretty sure she'd never make it home. She couldn't run. Oh, she had the money, but if the mob knew it was her, they would never stop looking. You know how it is. The money would run out soon enough, and there would always be someone affiliated with the mob who would find her. She was smart. She knew how things worked."

"If she were smart," Brody said, "she wouldn't have ripped off the mob."

The lawman ignored his comment. "When she got out of bed that morning, she only saw one solution."

"I was wrong," Brody said. "This is the part where her story goes bad."

Onderdonk pointed a finger and thumb at the big man and clicked his tongue, firing his pretend gun. "That morning, after Officer Daniel O'Leary put on his uniform and went to work, Evelyn Spier slipped into her best dress and walked into the local office of the FBI."

Chapter 21

There was another thump in the back of the store.

"Travis!" Brody yelled. "Wait here," he said to Onderdonk and hurried to the *Cozy* section. The cat wasn't anywhere he could find, but there were several piles of books he'd knocked to the floor. Brody collected them together and stuffed them on a shelf, not bothering to check if they were in the right spot.

When he returned to the front counter, the lawman had picked up the copy of *The Deep Blue Good-by*. Onderdonk's lips silently moved as he read the back jacket. "Travis McGee. Is that where you got the cat's name?"

"What about it?"

"Nothing. I didn't take you for a reader."

"I can read."

"I didn't say you couldn't, but back in Quantico, you said you didn't."

"Maybe I changed, or you underestimated me."

"Clearly."

"What happened with Evie when she turned herself in?"

Onderdonk carefully laid the paperback on the counter. "Just what you would expect. Initially, the agent on duty didn't believe her. Then she started dropping the names and dates of the people and places that Danny mentioned in his sleep. The agent wanted her to go home and told her someone would be in contact. Evie refused. She knew it was too dangerous to leave."

"Obviously," Brody said. "If she went home, she was a dead woman."

"She didn't give up though. She kept after it until they located an agent who was investigating the mob, and he took an interest in her. He listened to her story and realized what she had. After getting authorization to put her in a safe house, the agent and his team interviewed her in earnest. Initially, Evie didn't want to admit to the robberies she committed, but the names and dates of the mob hits had been printed in the newspaper. It wasn't enough to build a case around or to protect her.

"When she finally copped to the robberies, though, the game changed. The agent sent a couple of others to pick up her partners. That's when the proverbial sh—" Onderdonk paused, "stuff hit the fan."

Brody nodded his appreciation for Onderdonk's avoidance of swearing in his store.

The lawman continued. "The agents discovered some unknown men in broad daylight had already grabbed the first partner. That guy was never heard from again. Another group of unidentified men tried to grab the second partner, but he fought back. That man died in a gunfight. All a sudden, only Evelyn Spier was left to finger Daniel O'Leary."

"And she did?"

"She had to. What other choice did she have? If she went home, she was a dead girl. By this point, the mob and Danny Boy knew she was talking to the FBI. As for the G-Men, they had her pinned to the wall. She told them everything—everything Danny Boy did, everything she did, everything she ever saw at the club."

"I understand," Brody muttered. "I've been there."

"That's when the FBI agents caught a break and snatched O'Leary."

"They grabbed the dirty cop?" Brody asked.

Onderdonk nodded. "Once the man's girl was in the tank, his head was quickly put on the chopping block. The G-Men had wiretaps in various places around town and overheard an order to take out Danny Boy."

"Did he talk to the feds?

"He eventually did, but he didn't have to. Just having him inside caused the mob to go crazy. People were talking on the phone when they shouldn't have. Guys were getting clipped so they would keep their mouths shut. From what I read, the spring of seventy-nine was brutal for the coroner."

"Snitches get ditches," Brody said. He knew he still faced that ugly reality if anyone from the club ever found out where he was hiding.

"In the end, there were seventeen arrests, eleven convictions, and almost a dozen dead guys who were no longer playing in the cesspool."

"And you had to park Evie somewhere."

"Not me, I was still a kid, but yeah, the bureau agreed to give her protection which passed to us to provide. That's when we bought this store here. Before Evie got her hands on it, the place sold books for the hippie types. She was the one who made it a mystery bookstore."

"She was sent here in eighty-one?"

"January of eighty-one, to be exact. Almost forty years ago. I inherited her file when her original handler retired. She was an easy witness. She loved this town and this bookstore."

"You think this new restaurant around the corner, the one that's a front—"

Onderdonk interrupted by lifting a finger. "That you *suspect* is a front."

"That I *know* is a front."

"You don't know."

Brody's eyes slanted. "I know."

"Whatever."

"You think they could have something to do with her going missing?" Brody asked. "I mean, I would imagine they're connected to Boston, right? And we're talking the Chicago mob forty years ago. How would anyone even know?"

"The mob never forgets," Onderdonk said, his face solemn. "Besides, it's all about quid pro quo. You find one of their traitors; hopefully, they'll find one of yours."

"How would they even know to look for her or what she might look like?"

"They know," the marshal said flatly.

Brody laughed. "No, they wouldn't."

"Yes, they do."

"Really, Ted? Don't be obtuse." He hoped he was using the word correctly.

Onderdonk rolled his eyes. "They use a little thing called the Internet, Beau. Ever hear of it?"

Brody scrunched his face, but quickly relaxed when he noticed Onderdonk had pulled back as if he was regretting the words he had just uttered. "What is it?"

"Nothing." The marshal suddenly seemed anxious.

"Yeah, there is something. You got all weird like you're holding something back. What is it?"

The lawman closed his eyes and slowly inhaled. While he thought, he nodded several times to himself.

"Don't mess with me," Brody said. "If it's bad news, tell me."

Onderdonk opened his eyes and said, "Start your computer."

The big man turned to the keyboard on the counter and tapped the spacebar, which brought the monitor to life.

"Open the browser and type this in."

When Brody was ready, Onderdonk slowly said, "www dot the FBI is a bunch of dirty rats dot com."

Brody did so with only his index fingers. Onderdonk watched in fascination as Brody hunted and pecked his way around a keyboard.

"Good lord, man, how do you ever get anything done on a computer?"

"We hardly ever used them. If we needed something, the prospects or one of the girls did it."

A nearly blank page popped up with only space for a username and password.

"Type in user where it says username," the lawman said.

Brody's eyes slanted.

"Trust me," Onderdonk said.

The big man's two fingers typed in the word. "Let me guess. The password is *password*."

"You're a genius. Type it in."

Brody stared at the marshal.

"We have a hacker in the WitSec program. He helps us out. We found out about this site, and he got us access."

Brody typed in *password*, and a new screen greeted him.

Emblazoned across the top of the monitor was FBI Rats.

Leaning in close to study the screen, he whispered, "What is this?"

"This is the mob's repository of all their missing people. This is where they list those we've put into the Witness Protection Program."

"You're kidding."

"I wouldn't do that. There are some listed we aren't protecting, but they believe we are. Why would we correct that mistaken assumption, right?"

Brody glanced up to the marshal.

"Type in Evelyn Spier," Onderdonk said.

He turned his attention to the computer but hesitated from typing. The words FBI RATS mocked him from the monitor. He swallowed and licked his lips. Then he looked down at the keyboard. Brody's two fingers jumped around the keyboard.

When Evelyn's profile popped up, there was a photograph of her from the late seventies as well as a computer-manipulated photo to make her appear older. He tapped an altered photo. "Is that her?"

"Not exactly. That's their attempt to show what she might look like now. It's a pretty good representation though. Her hair is shorter and grayer, but it's actually quite close."

Brody studied the picture. "That's Alice, huh?"

"We monitor her profile here. If they remove it, we'll know for certain that she's dead. As long as it remains up, that means they're still looking for her, too."

His eyes moved to the marshal. "You're not sure she's dead?"

Onderdonk shook his head. "She may be. Perhaps she went for a walk and got hit by a car, and no one has found her yet. We don't know that the mob is involved with her disappearance." He pointed at the screen. "But if that profile comes down, we'll know they have verified she's dead."

Brody crossed his arms and returned to studying the computer screen. "Is that why you allow this site to exist? Shouldn't you take it down?"

"First of all, this falls into the gray area of freedom of the press. As a law enforcement agency, we would have to tread very lightly on pulling something like this down. Second, they're not advertising this site. It doesn't pop up on any Google searches. Most of all, we like being able to monitor what they're doing and what they think our people look like."

Brody leaned forward and let his two fingers type in a once-familiar name. He hoped nothing would pop up, suspecting nothing would. The Satan's Dawgs rarely had contact with the mafia. On the rare occasions they did, it was to provide interference on transport jobs the Italians were doing.

When the picture of him with long hair and a beard appeared on the monitor, under the site's banner, he felt a clutching around his heart. There was no escaping the truth of the matter.

Beau Smith, the former bookkeeper for the Satan's Dawgs, had officially been branded an FBI Rat.

"This is not good," he muttered.

The website listed his physicals. Six foot four. Two hundred twenty-five pounds. Blonde hair. Blue eyes. It showed various photos of the tattoos on his hands, his chest, and his back.

Brody turned to Onderdonk, whose face remained passive. When the big man turned back to the computer, he scrolled down to find additional pictures of himself with various haircuts.

One photo showed him bald. It would have been funny if it wasn't being used for people to hunt him.

Another replaced his blonde mane and beard with short black hair and a mustache. He looked like an angry plumber.

Yet another photo showed him with a spiky haircut and a five o'clock shadow. The portrait made him look like he was ready for a day playing beach volleyball.

It was the final picture, though, that gave him pause. In it, Beau Smith's long blonde hair was trimmed to a friendly businessman's cut, and his unruly beard was entirely shaved off to reveal flawless skin underneath. It looked like Brody Steele was staring into a mirror.

His mouth slowly dropped open, and he turned to Onderdonk.

"As I said, Beau, we do our best to monitor this site."

Brody crossed his arms and stared at the computer screen. "This should come down."

"It's a tactical play."

He lowered his head in thought.

"I'll look into the Italians," Onderdonk said. "I'll bring Ekleberry into it as well. The mob is the FBI's territory. Everything will be all right."

Brody slowly rubbed both hands over his face then looked up at the marshal. "You should also look into a body found in Massabesic Lake."

"Where's that?"

"Down in New Hampshire, near Manchester. There was an article in the newspaper a couple of days ago. An elderly woman was shot in the back of the head, and her fingers were snipped off."

"Sounds like a professional job," Onderdonk said.

"If it was, it was sloppy."

"You still have that paper?" the lawman asked.

"No, but I read about it while I was at the Italian restaurant."

"Huh," Onderdonk grunted.

"That's what I thought."

"I'll look into it and get back to you."

"When Alice went missing," Brody asked, "what did you do with her car?"

"We never found it," Onderdonk said.

"What about the furniture in her apartment? It's pretty empty. Did you guys come in and clean it out?"

"That we did take. A crew came in at night and pulled everything out for forensic analysis. We'll bring some new stuff in for you."

"And no one saw you?"

Onderdonk shrugged. "This town rolls up the sidewalks at eight p.m. It wasn't hard to do for some professionals."

Brody stared at his picture on the computer monitor. "You've got me here like a worm on a hook."

"It's okay, Brody. No one knows you're here. Besides, we're watching you."

"But weren't you watching Alice, too?"

Onderdonk didn't answer. He merely rapped his knuckles on the counter and gave Brody a comradely nod before he left the shop. On the way out, he let the bell ding.

Chapter 22

He was out back, looking at the rusty 1985 Ford he'd received from the WitSec program.

Maybe he should just jump in and run to someplace far from Pleasant Valley. Brody ruefully shook his head. Everything seemed far away from Maine, but the most northeastern state in the U.S. really wasn't the problem.

He couldn't go into the heartland of America where there were brother chapters of the Satan's Dawgs everywhere. Every state had a group friendly to the Dawgs, except Minnesota. For whatever reason, the Dawgs never made a connection in The Gopher State. No one in the crew wanted to go there anyway.

Briefly, he played with the idea of racing down the east coast until he arrived in sunny Fort Lauderdale, the home of Travis McGee. But there were plenty of motorcycle chapters along the way friendly to the Dawgs.

Even if he chose to flee his country and run to Canada, the Dawgs knew clubs up there, too. Besides, Canada itself was simply a miserable idea. Winter, hockey, and Tim Horton's donuts were the only things Brody equated with the Great White North, and he hated all three. Canada was essentially North Minnesota.

He put his arms on the edge of the truck and rested his head on the back of his hands.

Maine seemed the right choice for a hiding place. There wasn't a brother chapter this far north. As far as he knew, no one in the club had ever been to the state. *Why would they?*

Even if Onderdonk was using him as bait, Pleasant Valley made a good home.

Brody wondered if Evie Spier had any similar thoughts as she transformed herself into Alice Walker.

The building's rear door squeaked as it was pulled open. Brody glanced over his shoulder to see Daphne Winterbourne standing there.

"There you are," she said.

He turned around and leaned against the truck. "Here I am."

"No one is handling the shop."

"That is true," Brody agreed.

"Aren't you worried someone will steal something?"

"If someone is going to steal a book, let them. Maybe it will stop them from doing something stupid later on." At that moment, Brody wondered if he had read more as a kid, would his life have been different?

"Are you okay?" Daphne asked, stepping toward him.

"Sure."

"You seem sad."

"I'm good." He lifted his face to the sun to try and cut through his depression. Even the presence of the lovely Daphne Winterbourne didn't cheer him up.

"I wanted to say thank you for a lovely evening last night."

He dropped his chin and forced a smile.

"Really," she said, returning his smile. "I had such a wonderful time. I'm hoping we can do it again."

"I'd like that."

"What are you doing tonight? I'll cook for you."

"Tonight? Isn't that a bit forward?"

The smile faded from Daphne's lips. "I'm sorry."

"I was joking. Tonight will be perfect."

"Great," she said, her smile returning. "Do you remember where I live?"

"I can find it in the dark."

"You won't have to. Dinner at six-thirty. Okay?"

"Perfect," he said again.

"Want to walk me back to the grocery store?"

They went most of the way in silence, each stealing glances at the other, smiling when caught. It was only a couple of blocks, but Brody enjoyed the quiet time with her. When they were about a block away, Daphne slid her hand into his.

Herb Paxton, the older man from the breakfast diner, approached them on the sidewalk. He scowled at Brody as he passed. That was a response with which he was familiar.

When they arrived at the front of The Pleasant Peasant, Daphne turned and faced him.

"You left the store open," she said.

"I know, but it was more important to spend time with you."

Her eyes softened, and she pursed her lips together for a moment. Then she leaned in and kissed him on the cheek.

"See you tonight," she said and hurried inside the store.

***

He didn't walk back to the store so much as he floated on air. Brody had never felt this way toward a woman. His relationships with the opposite sex had always tended to more transactional—momentary interludes and short-term associations he knew would end badly. At the time, he thought it was a great way to live. Not tied down and free to roam wherever he wanted. Now, he was sure he didn't want to do that anymore.

Some of the guys in the MC had old ladies, but they were not wives molded by society's expectations any more than their husbands were. Traditional spouses were committed to each other. In the club, the men dedicated themselves to the Dawgs first, and their old ladies came a distant second. That was normal behavior in the MC. It would be considered abnormal conduct in Pleasant Valley.

Being away from the club gave him a different perspective on life. Meeting Daphne added to how he felt. He was smitten with her, of course, but Brody thought it was more the town that was changing his perception. Around Pleasant Valley, the various couples, regardless of their age, seemed content. The relationships appeared peaceful and happy. They weren't teased for being in love and for wanting to be solely with the other person.

His quiet contemplations were interrupted by the sound of a woman yelling, "Oh," from behind him. Even before he turned around, he heard heavy breathing and the sounds of physical exertion.

Constable Emery Farnsworth slammed on the brakes of his bicycle, skidding its rear tire outward in a half-moon arc toward Brody's feet. His eyes were hidden behind a pair of cycling glasses. His face was red from exertion.

Brody stood still with his eyes locked onto the Pleasant Valley cop. When the bicycle's rear tire lightly touched his foot, he playfully said, "Ouch."

Farnsworth's lip curled, and he said, "There's more where that came from."

"Really?" Brody said, grabbing the handlebars of the bike.

The officer tried to yank the bike free from the big man's grasp but was unable.

"Let go," Farnsworth commanded.

"You hit me with your bike. I think you should fill out an accident report. Maybe call the chief."

At the mention of his boss, Farnsworth stopped tugging on the handlebars. "Hey, now. Is that really necessary?"

"What would he say about your threat of brutality?"

"I didn't threaten you."

"You said there's more where that came from. That's an implied threat. I would know. I've said that sort of thing, too."

Farnsworth looked away.

"Is this about Daphne?" Brody asked.

"No," Farnsworth muttered.

"Did you just see us outside the grocery store?"

The officer turned back to Brody and removed his sunglasses in a snatching motion. His eyes burned with anger, but he kept his comments to himself.

Brody stared at the bicycle cop. He was perfectly suited for Pleasant Valley. If Farnsworth were a policeman anywhere else, he would have been eaten alive within his first ten minutes on the street. He let go of the bike.

"I'm sorry about Daphne, Emery, but she's not your girlfriend anymore."

The officer's eyes lowered to the ground.

"There's got to be other girls in this town for you to go out with."

"Not like Daphne."

Brody couldn't argue that.

Farnsworth wiggled the handlebars back and forth. He mumbled, "You might have messed up my alignment."

"Can I ask you a police question?"

The officer smirked for a second, then relaxed his lips and nodded. "Ayuh," he softly said.

"Alice Walker."

"What about her?"

"When she went missing, did you report it to anyone?"

"She's not missing though. You bought the business from her."

Brody snapped his fingers. "Right. But before I bought it, when everyone first thought she was missing, people came to you asking about her disappearance."

"Ayuh, many people did."

"What did you do?"

"I checked the store, and I went into her apartment."

"You went inside?"

"Ayuh, she didn't keep it locked."

"Huh."

"She wasn't there, so I filed a missing person's report."

"And that's it?"

"We've nevah had anyone go missing before, and no one was asking us to do more."

Brody crossed his arms, lost in thought.

"But everything worked out okay. Alice turned up and sold her business."

He studied the cop. "That's right, Emery. Everything turned out okay."

"You're not going to tell the chief about this, right?"

Brody shook his head. "No, we're cool."

Farnsworth slipped his sunglasses back on then lifted the front of his bicycle around the big man. "I need to get my alignment checked," he muttered.

The officer climbed onto his bike and slowly pedaled away.

Chapter 23

Brody had just finished a phone call when Donna Columbo entered the store and paused at the entry. Her right hand held the front door open, and her left hand rested on her hip. She wore a black blouse unbuttoned dangerously low, bright pink shorts, and black high heels. Her platinum hair was piled on top of her head. Slung over her shoulder was a giant Louis Vuitton purse.

"You're letting the humidity in," Brody said.

She stood there a couple of seconds longer, like a bratty teenager refusing to be told what to do. Reluctantly, she stepped inside and released the door, letting it slowly close behind her. The bell once again chimed its warning.

Donna stalked around to the counter and cocked a hip. "Well?" she said seductively.

"Well, what?"

"Ain't ya gonna say I look nice?"

She looked like a walking, talking slab of Neapolitan ice cream. In his former life, he would have said she looked good enough to eat in hopes it led to someplace dangerous. With thoughts of Daphne and socially acceptable relationships creeping into his dreams, he kept that inappropriate comment to himself. Besides, he didn't want to encourage the wife of a mob boss.

"You look nice," Brody said, his tone flat and noncommittal.

"Damn straight, I look nice."

"Did you dress up to come to the bookstore?"

"You wish. For your information, I look good every day."

Brody crossed his arms. "What can I do for you, Donna?"

"Aww, you remembered my name," she said, a smile playing across her lips.

"And I remember your husband's."

"Oh, *him*."

"Yeah, him."

Travis wandered out of the *Noir* aisle and sat in the middle of the floor, studying the visitor. Brody watched him, which caused Donna to turn and casually inspect the feline. When she again faced Brody, she said, "He doesn't like you very much."

"Who? The cat?"

"No, ya dingbat. My husband."

"He probably saw you making googly eyes at me at the restaurant."

"That's not why. Jimmy was telling him how you was disrespectful and all."

"Jimmy? Is that the weightlifter?"

"Yeah, Jimmy De Luca. We call him Jimmy the Pump because of how much time he spends in the gym."

"Jimmy the Pump? Gross."

"He's sorta soft up here," she said, tapping the side of her head. "Like he's stuck in high school or somethin'."

"How was he after our fight?"

"You two had a fight?" That information seemed to brighten Donna further. "Who won?"

"You'll have to ask him."

She studied Brody's face. "I'm gonna guess you got the better end. You're still handsome, and Jimmy ain't much of a fightah. He's built for intimidation."

Travis sneezed and ran a paw over his face.

Donna turned and looked at the cat. "He's sort of a weird fella, ain't he?"

"He grows on you."

"Ugh." She faced Brody. "So, where do you live, sailah?"

"Not around here."

Her smile faded. "Is it fah?"

"I drive in every day. Hours each way."

Suspicion clouded her face. "Hmm."

"You going to buy a book, Donna?"

Her face scrunched. "Uh, no."

"Then why did you stop by?"

"I told you I'd be back, but clearly, you're not buying what I'm selling."

"No, ma'am, I am not."

"It's that woman you were with at the restaurant. Who is she?"

"Does it matter?"

"You bet it does. I want to know my competition. Is she your girlfriend?"

"Maybe."

"We're getting ready to leave this town, but when I come back, I'm gonna do something about that."

"What are you going to do?"

"I don't know yet, but I'll think of somethin'."

Donna walked to the door then, pulled it open, and held it there. She turned around and watched the big man, not saying anything.

"The humidity," Brody said, knowing it wouldn't make a difference.

"I'm like the Canadian Mountaineers," Donna announced, "I always get my man."

"That's the Mounties," he said, remembering the *Dudley Do-Right* cartoons he'd watched as a child at his grandmother's. "And I don't think that's really their motto." At least, that's what his grandmother had told him.

"What?" she said, scrunching her face.

"It's the Mounties," he repeated. "Not the Mountaineers."

Donna rolled her eyes. "Just because you own a mystery bookstore doesn't mean you know everything about genealogy."

She spun then, letting go of the door, and left in a huff.

The bell rang as the door closed.

***

He looked up from *The Deep Blue Good-by* when the brass bell dinged again. Brody was surprised to see the waiter from the Italian restaurant enter the store. When the two made eye contact, the older man rolled his lips inward and nodded politely.

"Anything I can help you with?" It was a question clerks had asked him throughout the years. He felt funny saying it since he didn't know anything about the store and knew even less about mystery books.

The man shook his head and moved deeper into The Red Herring.

Brody returned his attention to his book. A couple of times, he looked up to catch the older man peering in his direction. The waiter would hurriedly look away, embarrassed at being caught.

When it happened for the third time, Brody put his paperback down and approached the man. "Is there something I can help you with, pops?" He wondered if he'd been sent to spy on him by Frankie Columbo.

The older man appeared frail next to the much larger bookstore owner. He slowly said, "Looking for the books."

"*The* books? Which books?"

The older man pulled a small piece of paper from his pocket. On it, in obviously feminine handwriting, was the name Raymond Chandler followed by several book titles: *The Big Sleep*, *The Little Sister*, and *The Long Goodbye*. Brody relaxed then. Chloe Columbo must have written these titles down for him.

"You're looking for these?"

"*Si.*"

Brody smiled and patted the older man's shoulder. "All right, pops. Let's see if we can find them."

The waiter nodded and followed Brody as they moved through the various aisles. They started in the *Cozy* aisle, walked through the *Thriller* row, and eventually found the titles in the one labeled *Classics*.

"You're in luck," Brody said, pulling the three novels from a shelf. "These look to be the only Raymond Chandler books I have."

"Lucky," the waiter agreed.

Brody handed two of them to the older man but held on to *The Big Sleep*. He flipped it over and read the back of it. "Philip Marlowe, huh? These any good?"

"Excuse?"

"These books. Are they good?"

The older man shrugged. "Do not know. Learn the English from reading."

"You read books to learn English?"

"*Si.*"

Brody handed the man the last Chandler novel and returned to the front. The older man followed him and put the books on the counter.

"Anything else?" the big man asked.

The waiter shook his head.

Brody checked the back of the books and quickly announced a total. The older man pulled several bills from his pocket and handed him the exact amount. He slid the three novels from the counter, nodded politely, said "*Arrivederci,*" and left the store.

He tucked the bills into the cash register, not because he knew what he was doing, but because it seemed like what he should be doing.

For a moment, he wondered if he should learn how to order replacements for the Chandler novels. If those were the last ones, it probably meant they were popular among Pleasant Valley readers.

Instead of learning how to place the order though, he returned to the Travis McGee adventure.

Chapter 24

He was on a knee in the *True Crime* aisle, retrieving several books Travis had knocked over, when he smelled the aroma of the ocean. Brody paused and listened. He became aware of the change in humidity within the store.

Someone got inside without the little bell ringing. Quietly, he stacked the books on the nearest shelf. He snuck out the back of the aisle, hoping to surprise whoever was standing in the store.

But there was no one.

He reached up to stroke his beard, the one that he'd shaved off days ago. In a mixture of disappointment and frustration, his hand dropped to his side.

When the store's rear door clicked shut, his head snapped in its direction. He quickly moved down the back hallway.

As he passed the restroom, he glanced in and confirmed no one was there.

Next, Brody paused at the basement stairs and saw they were still locked. No one could have gotten in from down there.

He shoved the back door open, but there wasn't anyone in the alley either.

He glanced up the stairs to his apartment. No one was at his door, and he had locked it when he left in the morning.

Maybe he was losing his mind, he thought.

He looked up and down the alley a final time and pulled the door closed, securing it.

As he returned to the front of the store, he smelled the ocean air and felt the humidity again. He reasoned it was because he had opened the back door. However, Brody tossed that line of thought aside when he saw Special Agent Max Ekleberry standing in the middle of his shop, a hard-sided briefcase in hand.

"Were you just in here?" Brody asked.

Ekleberry held a single finger to his lips. After placing the briefcase on the counter, he removed a device that resembled a small viewfinder. The agent held it to his eye and looked about the store. Slowly and carefully, he stepped into different locations of the shop, his eye scanning everything. When he finished, he returned to the counter. He carefully placed the piece of equipment into the hard case and next removed an item that bore a resemblance to a child's walkie-talkie.

The special agent then wandered about the store lifting the device over various surfaces and items. His eyes locked onto the readings of the little handheld device. After covering every inch of the store, Ekleberry returned to his briefcase. Brody started to say something, but the agent slowly shook his head and again raised a single finger to his lips.

The lawman now traded the walkie-talkie device for a black wand, the size of a small flashlight. He retraced his steps, lifting his hand over every surface and item. When he was satisfied, he clicked off the wand and walked back to his briefcase.

"Go ahead," Ekleberry said. "Your store is clean."

"Were you just in here?"

"I did a pass-through," he said, packing away the little wand. "Then looped around the front to see if I had been followed."

"Were you?"

Max shook his head.

"Why are you worried about being followed?"

"Onderdonk called and said he thought the mob was in town."

"He say anything else?"

"He told me everything. I think he's getting ahead of the mess of trouble that's about to come his way."

"He told you about his missing witness?"

"The woman? Alice Walker? Yeah, he filled me in."

"He's using me as bait."

"I figured something was off when he sent you here."

Brody studied the man. He seemed genuine, but it was hard to tell with cops. They used lies to coerce confessions, which meant they had a built-in excuse for their untruths. Once that became ingrained into their belief system, cops often became better liars than the criminals they chased.

"I figured if the mob had any idea you were linked to the marshals and us, they might be listening and watching, but you're clean. We can go upstairs and check out your apartment if you want."

"In a minute."

Ekleberry leaned against the counter. "You called and left a message for me."

"I wanted to talk about Onderdonk, but it seems you two are already talking."

"Don't get your panties in a bunch, Beau."

"It's Brody," he said. "And I'm feeling like shark chum."

"That's because you are." There was no humor in Ekleberry's statement. "I don't like what Onderdonk did. It was a jerk move, but I can get you out of here. I'll get you another witness inspector, and they'll get you another town."

The agent's words should have brought him relief. Initially, he didn't want to be in this sleepy little town. He wanted to be where there was vibrancy and things to do. But Pleasant Valley had snuck up on him. He knew a lot of it had to do with a particular bookkeeper at the local grocery store.

"Not yet," Brody said.

Ekleberry tilted his head.

"Let's play this out."

"I can't force you to leave, Beau. You've held up your end of our bargain, but this isn't smart. If that truly is the mob and they find out you're an informant, well, you can imagine where this goes."

"This is Pleasant Valley. What are they going to do? Shoot up the town?"

The agent shrugged. "Who knows with these guys?"

Brody set his jaw. "I'm staying. I don't want to run. I like it here."

Ekleberry folded his arms. "Maybe you should tell me where this mob joint is and what you know."

Brody settled onto the stool behind the counter. "It's called Il Cuoco Irato," he began, and he proceeded to tell the agent everything he could remember.

Chapter 25

Carrie Fenton was an attractive woman in her late thirties. She wore a sleeveless white blouse with blue jean shorts and flip-flops. Tied on top of her head was a red bandana. A portion of her golden-brown hair slipped free in front of her forehead.

While her right arm was bare, tattoos covered her left.

Brody had called and left a message for her just as Donna Columbo had entered his store. He expected Carrie to call him back, not to walk into his shop confidently.

After introducing herself, Carrie studied him the same way a cop would—with distrust.

"You could have called," Brody said.

"I wanted to see you in person." Her eyes were curious behind red-lensed sunglasses.

"Yeah? Why?"

She set her notepad on the edge of the counter. "We'll get to that in a minute."

"How about we get to it now? I called you, remember?"

"How'd you get my number?" Carrie asked. Her voice was full of suspicion.

He pointed to the yellow sticky note on the computer. "Alice left it there."

Carrie leaned over the counter to look. She smelled like coconut butter. When she dropped back into place, she said, "Your message said you wanted to talk about Alice. So talk."

"One of the locals told me that you and Alice were friendly."

"What about it?"

"I'm trying to figure out what happened to her."

Carrie's left eyebrow raised. "Why do you care?"

"Because I do. I like the people around here, and they seem to like Alice."

"She was well-liked," Carrie agreed, "but that still seems like a strange reason for you to get involved. You don't know her. What's in it for you?"

Brody knew she wasn't a cop, but she certainly had the mannerisms and the tone of one.

"Give me something better than she was well-liked, or I'm out of here," she demanded.

"Excuse me?"

"Listen. My friend has been missing for weeks, and I'm worried about it. Then you call wanting to talk. I don't know you. And the only reason you're giving me is that Alice was well-liked. I'm not buying it. Give me something better, or I'm gone."

Carrie stepped back from the counter and took a step toward the door.

"There's a girl," Brody said.

"A girl?"

"She's a friend of Alice's, and she's upset that she's missing."

Carrie pursed her lips in thought. "What girl?"

"You wouldn't know her."

"I don't care. Tell me her name."

Brody had no idea why she was so argumentative with him, so he went on the offensive. "As Alice's friend, I'd figure you would want to know what happened to her."

"I do want to know. I've tried reaching her for weeks. No response."

Brody crossed his arms. "You've been looking for her?"

"Of course. I want to know why she took off. It's not like her to disappear. In the whole time I've known her, she never really left Pleasant Valley. Maybe for an afternoon, sometimes a day, but never overnight."

"How long is that?"

"Year and a half, maybe."

Brody didn't believe her. The way she talked about her friendship with Alice seemed fishy, almost forced. "You're an unlikely friendship."

"What's that supposed to mean?"

"The age difference. She could be your mom."

"People can't be friends if they aren't age-appropriate? That's ageism."

Brody sighed. "That's not what I meant."

"It can't be taken any other way."

"I'm trying to understand what you two were doing together."

Carrie looked around and extended her arms wide. "Books, man. She owned a bookstore. I'm a writer." She pointed to the display of her books. "Those are mine over there."

"Yeah, I know. I haven't sold any, by the way."

"Ouch."

Brody stared at her. He didn't want to argue with the woman. He really was trying to determine what happened to Alice. "I'm sorry. That was a cheap shot."

She glanced at her books. "Maybe it's the display."

"Maybe," Brody agreed.

The cat made his way out then and saw Carrie. He immediately walked over and rubbed himself against her leg. She reached down and petted the cat. "Hiya, Sherlock."

"You want the cat?"

Carrie frowned. "He's a bookstore cat. You're clearly new to the industry. I think it's a law or something that every independently owned bookstore needs to have a cat."

"If it were a requirement to have a cat, I wouldn't have bought the place. I don't even feed him, and he stays here."

"You're not feeding him?

"I'm hoping he'll run away and join the circus."

"How's that working?"

"It's only been a few days. Give it time."

"It's okay, Sherlock," she cooed, rubbing his ear. "I'll bring you some vittles the next time I see you."

"What were you doing with Alice?" Brody asked.

Carrie reached for her notebook and pulled it from the counter. "Does it matter?"

"Maybe," Brody said. "I don't know. My friend said whenever you two were together, it looked like you two were conspiring."

"Do you think she's in danger?" Carrie asked, ignoring his question.

"She's missing. No one has heard from her in weeks now. That sounds like she could be in danger. Could she have run off with her foreign boyfriend?"

"What? No!"

"So, she has a foreign boyfriend."

"How would I know?"

"You responded as if she did, and you knew about it."

"No, I didn't."

"Yes, you did."

"No. I most certainly did not."

Brody stared at her for a moment then crossed his arms. He didn't know what game she was playing, but he was about to be done.

The woman tapped her notebook into her palm while she thought. She said, "I'm going to ask you something, and I don't want you to get offended."

"I won't promise that."

Carrie put her free hand on her hip. "Then I won't ask."

Brody smirked. "Fine. I promise not to get mad."

"You're lying."

"I swear."

"You said you were looking into Alice's disappearance for a girl."

"That's right."

"Let's assume I believe that. Why are you here? *Really* here, I mean."

"What?"

Carrie took a deep breath and studied him once more. Then she asked, "Are you the law?"

She thinks I'm a cop. The idea almost made Brody smirk.

Before he could think up a witty response, she asked, "Are you with the feds?"

Brody blinked several times. *How could she possibly know?*

"No," Brody said. "I'm just a bookstore owner. What makes you think I'm with the law?"

Carrie glanced around. She seemed unsure of herself now. "If you're not with the law, then are you in..."

"In what?" Brody asked, afraid to hear her finish her question.

"The program?"

Brody's heart raced.

The woman leaned in and whispered. "Alice was in the Witness Protection Program. Since she was, I'm guessing that means you are, too."

The big man's tongue felt thick, and he had trouble swallowing.

Carrie nodded with satisfaction. "Yeah, you're in the program."

"I'm not in any program."

"I don't believe you."

"How do you know that about Alice?" he croaked.

"I discovered it." Carrie was smiling now.

"*You* discovered it? How does something like that happen?"

"By accident. I was doing some research for a book about a mafia snitch in Portland."

"Oregon?" As soon as he said it, he felt like a fool.

Carrie tilted her head. "No, Maine."

"I know," Brody muttered.

Behind her rose-colored glasses, the woman rolled her eyes. "It's our largest city."

"I said, I *know*."

"It's less than an hour from here. It's a big city with about 70,000 people."

"That's not a big city."

Her shoulders slumped. "There's almost half a million in the Portland metro area."

"A metro area doesn't make it a big city."

Carrie gnawed her lip. "You argue too much to be the law."

Brody shrugged. "I never said I was."

"Then you're in the program. I don't care what you say."

"You got it wrong," he said with a shake of his head. "I'm just a guy running a bookstore."

Carrie's eyes went to the John D. MacDonald novel on the counter. "Okay, bookseller, name three other titles in the Travis McGee series."

"Excuse me?"

Smelling blood in the water, she said, "Or give me a recommendation of two similar writers from the same period. I'll give you a hint—it was the seventies."

Brody stared at her.

Sensing victory, she said, "Or give me a recommendation for other crime fiction stories that take place in Florida."

He crossed his arms and scowled.

Carrie flipped open her notepad and wrote something.

"What are you doing?" Brody asked.

"I'm jotting down your description, so I won't forget."

"Why?"

"Because I'm going to do some research on you when I get home. If you're not going to tell me who you are, then I'll find out myself."

Good luck with that, Brody thought.

He remained silent for a moment while Carrie finished her notes. When she was done, she said, "By the way, you never let me finish my story about the mafia snitch in Portland. Before you say there is no mafia in Maine, they're in any big city."

He opened his mouth to protest, but Carrie continued.

"The focus of my story—"

"The protagonist," Brody interrupted.

Her brow furrowed, and she waited.

"Sorry," he said. "Go ahead."

The writer nodded appreciatively and continued. "He entered witness protection and disappeared for several years."

"What did this guy do for the mob?"

"Are you going to interrupt every time I say something?"

"No," Brody said. This woman frustrated him.

"The man was an analyst."

"An analyst? What did he analyze?"

"Data, of course. He analyzed data." She sounded annoyed.

Brody's face warmed.

"Anyway, he called me one day and asked me to tell his story."

"A guy who is in the Witness Protection Program called *you* to tell *his* story. Why would he do that?"

She tossed her notepad on the counter. "Because I've written a series of True Crime novels set in Maine. He believed his former employers were about to get to him, and he wanted to get his story out before it was too late."

"Why did he think they were going to find him?"

"You're still interrupting," Carrie said.

Brody shrugged.

"I asked him the same thing, and he said he would tell me if we met. Of course, I wanted to hear his story, but I had to verify he wasn't some random creeper. He told me his real name, so I researched that part of him. I discovered his backstory was real, and we agreed to meet. He wouldn't reveal where he lived, and he wouldn't come to Maine, so we decided on Dayton. That would be Ohio if you didn't know."

"I knew that."

Carrie smirked. "Uh-huh. Anyway, we met at Denny's restaurant, and he began laying out his story. It was typical *Law & Order* stuff. Mob employee sees things he shouldn't. He then has a case of the guilts. The FBI gets their hooks into him, and he turns. They slap him into the Witness Protection Program, and he disappears."

"Typical," Brody murmured.

"Except this guy is an analyst, and he knew extra things about the mob most people wouldn't."

"Like what?"

Carrie leaned in. "Do you know they maintain a website that tracks all of the snitches who have ever ratted on them?"

She nodded with excitement as Brody realized what she was saying.

"Pretty crazy, huh?"

"Yeah," the big man muttered, "crazy."

"Anyway, he shows me this website. Its URL. That's the name of the website by the way—"

"I know.

"Just making sure. You don't look like the technologically savvy type. Anyway, the URL is so simple I wouldn't forget it. He tells it to me during his story and even gave me a username and password for it. After we met, I went home and entered it into Google. It didn't pop up in the search engine. Then I typed it into the address bar just as he said it. Boom, there it was. This whole website tracks all the FBI snitches who have disappeared into the protection program. It was crazy."

"Crazy," Brody repeated.

"There wasn't much history on any of the people listed. It wasn't a website for visitors, you know. It was a site used for catching rats."

"Rats," the big man muttered.

"You know, snitches."

"I know what a rat is."

"So I'm sitting in my hotel flipping through page after page of faces. According to my source, if a snitch dies, either from natural causes or, well, unnatural causes, their picture is removed. There is no fanfare, no bragging. Again, this site is not about the backstory and hyping the underworld's search for these people. It is totally about getting the information into the field.

"And I'm moving through these faces, and some of the pictures look old. I mean, like they were taken in the sixties and seventies. Someone has also done this very cool thing where they age the person in the photograph or modify their appearance slightly so you can imagine what they might look like today."

Brody stared at her, thinking about his own pictures on the website.

"I keep flipping through the pictures until I come to my source, Raymond Zambotti. I'm staring at his picture when I notice one of the photographs above it is someone I know very well."

Brody's eyes slanted, but he remained silent.

"You're going to make me say it, aren't you?"

He shrugged, trying to keep his expression non-committal.

"Before I go any further, I need to know that you're in the program. I can't share information about Alice that's confidential if I don't know that you're in the same situation as her."

"You've already told me that she's in the program. You've outed her. You're not a very good friend."

"Fine," Carrie said. "I'll take my notepad and go home where I'll confirm you're on this website. Then we'll finish this conversation."

Brody sighed. She was going to find out one way or another. Besides, he would rather have her on his side than angry with him. "I'm not a rat," he muttered.

"Does the mob think so?"

"I never did anything to the mob."

"Who did you snitch on?"

"My club."

"Your club? Wait. You don't have to tell me your story," Carrie said. "I don't want to know. You're here for a reason."

"So was Alice," Brody said.

"Right."

"And you want to find out what happened to her?"

"Sure," Carrie said, "that's why I'm here."

It didn't sound compelling to Brody.

"Are you really looking into Alice because of a girl?"

Brody nodded. "Yes. I like her, and she's upset about Alice."

"There's always a woman," Carrie said. "What's her name?"

He ignored the question again. "About Alice?"

"Alice," Carrie said and nodded. "Right. So I'm looking at Raymond Zambotti's picture, and who is staring back at me from just above it? Alice Walker. Although, she wasn't Alice Walker in that picture. She was a young woman named Evelyn Spier. There was a phone number to call if anyone saw her."

"Did you call that number?"

"No, I didn't call that number. Alice was my friend. What do you think I did?"

"I think you smelled a story, and you went right to her, maybe blackmailed her into telling you why she was on that website."

Carrie shook her head. "I didn't do that either. I told her what I saw, of course. How could I not? She closed the store early, and we went for a walk along the beach. She told me what happened back in Chicago during the last couple years of the seventies. That's when I asked if I could write her story."

"She wouldn't agree to that, would she?"

"She did so long as it would only be published after her death."

"Did you get that in writing?"

"Of course."

"And you have a finished manuscript?"

"It's almost done."

"It won't fit your Maine series since it's set in Chicago."

"Oh, it'll fit," she said. "I'm calling it *Lying in Maine*. I'm going to set it between idyllic scenes here in Pleasant Valley. It will work perfectly."

Brody crossed his arms, which drew Carrie's eyes to the tattoo on his hand.

"Fireball on back of the right hand," she said, then made an entry in her notebook.

"Do you have any idea where Alice is now?" he asked.

Her eyes flashed briefly away before settling back on Brody. "I've tried her cell phone and sent her emails. Those were the only ways I had to communicate with her. She never called me from the landline." Carrie pointed to the phone next to the computer. "After meeting her, I assumed she thought the place was bugged."

"It's not bugged," Brody said, confident after the search that Max Ekleberry had performed.

"I don't know how to get ahold of her beyond those two methods."

"If she's not found..." Brody said.

"I know. I've got a motive for her murder. The problem is I liked Alice, and we were friends."

"What happened to Zambotti, your original snitch?"

"He died before we could start the book."

"The mob found him?"

"No," Carrie said. "Simple heart attack. The man had a horrible diet."

"There you go."

"Was there anything else you wanted to ask me, Brody?"

"No," he said. "I got more than I bargained for with that call."

Carrie closed her notebook and studied the big man. "I think this is the start of a beautiful relationship."

"We don't have a relationship," Brody said, his face stern.

"Sure, we do," Carrie said, a smile spreading across her face. "I'm your customer now."

With that, she turned and left the store.

Chapter 26

The inside of her house was an explosion of colors. Brody wasn't sure he'd seen so many different hues in his life. One complete wall was painted in a variety of rectangles and squares, each a different color and separated by small white lines. The boxes were of various sizes.

All the other walls were a different solid color. It made for an unsettling experience.

He stared at the multi-colored wall for a moment, taking in the diversity of colored boxes.

"It's a little overwhelming, isn't it?" Daphne said.

"It's different," Brody admitted. "I've never seen anything like it."

"I started putting little samples on the wall to decide what color I wanted to paint it. Then I thought, why not do this?"

"It reminds me of the bus on *The Partridge Family*," Brody said.

"*The Partridge Family*? What's that?"

As a child, Brody watched the sickly-sweet sitcom while visiting his grandmother. He liked the songs that the family sang and had a crush on Laurie Partridge. He had never met a nice girl like that until Daphne.

"It was a television show from the early seventies. I used to watch the reruns whenever I visited my grandmother."

A white ceramic rhinoceros stood proudly on an end table. "What's with the rhino?" Brody asked.

"I thought it would be sort of cool to collect a whole zoo of these ceramic animals."

Brody lifted the heavy knickknack. It was larger than his hand, and the horn protruded several inches.

"But I only bought the rhinoceros then stopped."

"So you have a one-animal zoo," he said.

"Not very interesting, huh?"

"Not true. I find it kind of cute."

Did I really just say 'cute'? Brody thought. *What's happening to me?*

He carefully returned the rhino to the end table.

A beeping from the kitchen caused Daphne to hurry away. Brody followed her and watched as she turned off a timer then opened the open. She slipped on a couple of oven mitts and removed a casserole dish. Carefully, Daphne placed it on top of the stove. She also removed a loaf of French bread.

On the nearby table, two place settings were arranged.

"This is a spinach casserole," Daphne said as she scooped a portion of the casserole onto a plate.

"Spinach?" Brody asked.

"Trust me, it's good. It's my grandmother's recipe. Her mother created it after a visit to San

Francisco or thereabouts. Sometime in the thirties, I believe."

Brody lifted his plate and sniffed the odd-looking concoction.

"She called it Joe's Special. Some of the ladies in town have told me I make it wrong, that I should be using eggs, but I think it tastes fine as it is."

He watched her scoop a dollop of the casserole onto her plate. Then she cut a couple of pieces of bread for them.

"I'm sure it'll taste delicious." He did his best to sound convincing. He'd eaten some horrible things in his life. He was sure he could gut this down without much problem. The important thing was to make sure he showed Daphne how much he liked the casserole.

"This will sound weird," she said, opening the refrigerator, "but the secret to this is adding some ketchup. My grandfather used to slather it on. It gives it a nice kick."

Brody liked ketchup. He had grown quite fond of it while in juvenile detention and prison. He put it on most foods now.

In only a few moments, they were eating. The casserole was surprisingly good, especially with the added ketchup. It had been some time since Brody had a home-cooked meal. He ate faster than he expected, and when Brody finished, he looked up from a clean plate to see Daphne was only half-done with her meal. She smiled at him, pleased he'd eaten so much, so fast.

"It was fantastic," he said sheepishly. "What's in it?"

She made a strange face. "You really want to know? Ground beef, onions, and obviously spinach." Over the next several minutes, Daphne explained how to make the dish. When she finished telling him the recipe, she asked, "Want some more?"

"Definitely."

Daphne gave him another serving. This time Brody ate slower and enjoyed each bite.

With a fork, Daphne pushed her remaining casserole around her plate. "Where did she live?"

"*Who?*"

"Your grandmother. You said you watched that show with her. The one with the bus."

"She lived in Sioux City."

"That's Iowa, right?"

"Yeah."

"How often did you go there?"

"Whenever my mom had troubles."

"How often was that?"

"Every summer. Mom didn't want to spend three full months with me."

"That's terrible," Daphne said. Her fork hovered over her plate.

"It's okay. She wasn't that good of a mom."

"But your grandmother...?"

"She's the best person in the world."

"Your face brightens when you talk about her."

"When I would visit her," Brody said, "she made me feel special. Like I mattered. To my mom, I was a burden."

"Did you have a special name for your grandmother? I called mine Nana."

"Ma."

"Ma?"

"That's all anyone ever called her. Ma."

"What did you call your mom?"

"Paula."

"Oh."

Brody shrugged.

"What about brothers or sisters?"

"None."

"Your dad?"

"I never met him."

"That's sad."

"It's not so bad. From what my mom said, which wasn't much, he was a swindler with a messiah complex. He didn't stick around after she got knocked up. Ma refused to talk about him. Who knows how I would have turned out had he stayed?"

"You turned out fine without him," Daphne said. "Maybe it was for the best."

"Yeah," Brody muttered. "For the best."

"Do you still talk to Paula?"

"Haven't heard from her in years."

"That's sad."

"You already said that."

"I don't know what else to say."

"It's fine. Really. I stopped talking to her by the time I was in high school. We were essentially roommates then. We came to an uneasy agreement—I wouldn't interfere in her life if she didn't interfere with mine."

"And Ma?"

"I spent my summers with her, but as I got older, it got harder on her. I was a bit of troublemaker."

"You? You don't seem the type."

"You'd be surprised."

"Would I?"

"I was difficult for her. I was selfish."

"Isn't that how kids are?"

"Maybe. I don't know."

"What did she think about you joining the Navy?"

Brody paused. He didn't want to lie to Daphne any further. He wanted to tell her the truth, but he believed doing so would only lead to telling her everything. Then what would he do? And how would she react? Brody wasn't willing to risk everything at this moment. Besides, the truth could put her in jeopardy if anyone ever found out.

"Enough about my past," Brody said. "Let's talk about Alice Walker."

"Did you talk with the people who sold you the business?"

"I did."

"And?"

"They're going to get back to me."

"That's something, right?"

Brody nodded. "Have you ever met Carrie Fenton?" he asked.

"The author? Of course. Alice had her at the store for a signing."

"What did you think of her?"

"She was nice. I think she and Alice hit it off pretty well. Why do you ask?"

"She stopped by looking for Alice."

"And?"

"Carrie was... different. I got the feeling she was only telling me part of the truth."

"You think she was lying about something?"

"I'm not sure. It didn't feel like she was lying to me exactly, but it didn't feel like I was getting the whole truth either."

"Are you worried that you might have purchased the business under pretenses?"

Brody paused, considering how to answer. "I bought it through an online attorney. Everything should be okay."

"But no one knows where Alice is. It's all so... hinky."

"It has me concerned. I'll admit that. I want to make sure she's okay. Not only for you but so my being here is on the up and up."

"Is there anything I can do to help?"

"Did Alice ever mention seeing anyone?"

"You mean dating?"

"Yes."

"She didn't date anyone. Well, that's not true. When I was little, she was involved with a man named Gil. After he passed, she never was with anyone again."

"One of the ladies in her knitting circle said she mentioned seeing a foreigner."

"A foreigner?" Daphne asked. "I doubt it. She could barely stand the New England accent. How would she tolerate someone from another country?"

"People don't just disappear," Brody said. "And if they do, they've usually had help, whether they wanted it or not."

Daphne pondered his statement. "Maybe she rode off into the sunset. Like a cowboy in an old Western movie, but in a car, not on a horse. Why couldn't she have done something like that?"

Chapter 27

After dinner, Brody walked past Il Cuoco Irato. The *Open* sign was off, and the front lights were dimmed. Frankie Columbo was seated in the corner booth. He had a laptop open and a cell phone to his ear. The old waiter was dutifully cleaning the last few tables.

The big man watched for a few moments from a nearby tree. A boat's horn sounded in the distance. He waited for a little while longer, then stepped into the shadows and headed toward the shore. As he walked, he had the eerie sense of being followed. It was the same feeling he got a couple of nights ago when Jimmy the Pump had tailed him. He wondered if the man was trailing him again.

Brody stopped several times and stood still on the sidewalk. He turned around repeatedly, his eyes searching for anything moving in the darkness. Finally, his unease faded, and he continued his journey toward the beach. He heard another horn sound. This time it was further out in the bay.

At the beach, he found a shadowy area and waited. It didn't take long, and a small single-engine boat arrived. The ship ran aground with two men aboard. One of the men tossed a large duffel bag onto the beach which thudded when it landed. The man then jumped to the sand himself. His shoes, with the laces tied together, hung around his neck. He turned around and pushed the boat back into deeper water.

The figure walked through the sand until he reached the pathway. He sat and brushed off his feet. Then he put his socks and shoes on. The man wore black pants and a long dark shirt.

When he stood, the man secured the duffel bag over his right shoulder, then casually strolled up Main Street. By his walk, a confident gait, it was clear he wasn't concerned about being followed. He never looked back to see if anybody was nearby.

The man whistled as he walked up to Second Street, hung a right, and went directly to the Italian restaurant. Brody shadowed him the entire way. By the time he made it to his previous hiding spot to watch inside Il Cuoco Irato, the man and his duffel bag were gone. Only Frankie Columbo remained, his eyes intently studying his laptop.

***

Brody hid in the shadows for twenty minutes, watching Frankie the Dove until he decided it was time to go home. He slipped from the darkness and took the long way to The Red Herring. He still couldn't shake the feeling he had been followed earlier.

He could have gone around the back and into the alley, but he wanted to stop first and get his knitting kit. He was restless after dinner with Daphne and then seeing the shadowy figure with the duffel bag. A few minutes of knitting might help set his mind at ease.

He opened the front door to the bookstore and immediately locked it behind him. When he stepped into the darkness of the lobby, he sensed the movement too late.

It was too big and aggressive for the cat.

Something hit him under the chin, causing him to stumble backward into Carrie Fenton's book display. The cardboard tower collapsed under his weight. Brody clambered back to his feet as the shadow neared him.

"Time for some payback, rat," Jimmy the Pump said.

Rat?

The word still echoed in Brody's head as Jimmy punched him in the stomach, forcing the wind out and doubling him over. The weightlifter grabbed him and threw him into the wiry book spinner.

Brody landed on top of the device. Several of the book holders dug into his back. He grunted in pain and rolled to his hands and knees.

Jimmy De Luca was quick, not giving the big man a moment to recover. He kicked Brody under the armpit. The pain was excruciating, and Brody tucked his elbow tight to his side to limit further damage.

As he stood, The Pump grabbed Brody by his other arm and swung him into the front counter. The big man's stomach hit the edge, forcing him to expel his breath. In hopes of regaining both his balance and his wits, his hands slapped down on the counter.

When his fingers touched the knitting kit nearby, he instinctively clutched the needles and yarn into a fist.

"You fight like a rat," Jimmy said from behind.

Brody spun and stepped toward the weightlifter. De Luca hadn't expected it, and he raised his hands to protect his face. Brody's fist arced through the darkness and banged against Jimmy's chest, provoking a squeal from The Pump.

"What did ya do?" Jimmy yelped in agony as he stared down at the knitting needles protruding from his chest. Several rows of stitches hung precariously from the thin metal poles. A line of yarn ran to the skein on the counter.

Jimmy took a half-step back and dropped to a knee. He brought up both hands but stopped short of grabbing the two needles that extended from his chest.

Brody watched as Jimmy slowly fell to the ground. A few minutes later, he was silent.

The big man walked to the window and observed his surroundings for several minutes to see if anyone was outside. When he was satisfied that no one was moving, his heart rate slowed, and his breathing became even.

As he studied the body on the floor, Brody wondered how Jimmy had gotten into the store. The front door was locked when he entered. The big man walked to the rear of the store and found the backdoor slightly ajar. There was splintering around the lock. De Luca must have kicked it in, Brody decided. No one would have seen him do it due to the hedges lining the alleyway. The alley's privacy had backfired on him.

Brody returned to the lobby of his shop. He moved the spinner and books away from Jimmy's body. He then placed the yarn skein on top of the weightlifter's body. Carefully, he used the rug from the middle of the store to wrap up the dead man.

It was awkward lifting the load, but it wasn't the first time he had carried a dead body. It also wasn't the first time he'd moved a body in a rolled-up carpet. Once outside, he dropped the roll into the back of the dented F-150.

The only time he'd driven it was when he arrived in Pleasant Valley. He hoped it would start. Otherwise, he was going to have a lot of explaining to do.

Chapter 28

Brody was bent over, reinserting the last of the books into the spinner. He didn't know what order they were supposed to go in, so he placed them back in a way that would fill out the wire racks. When the brass bell chimed, it caused Brody's eyes to drift toward the store's entrance.

Standing in the doorway was Francis Columbo, affectionately known in the press as Frankie the Dove. The heavyset man wore a green tracksuit with a white stripe running down the arms and legs. His right pocket bulged in a distorted manner that wasn't from a wad of cash. On his head was a pageboy hat.

Columbo stepped into the store and stopped near the cardboard display for Carrie Fenton's books. It was crushed during the fight with Jimmy the Pump, but Brody had rebuilt it about an hour before Columbo's arrival. It required a significant amount of masking tape to repair the damage and now stood with a twisted lean.

"What happened here?" the Dove asked.

As he straightened, Brody said, "The cat."

"A cat did all this?" Columbo studied the mangled display. "Must be a big, f—"

"He is," Brody interrupted. "He's a menace."

Something thumped in the back of the store.

Columbo's head snapped toward the direction of the noise, and his eyes searched for movement. "What was that?" he said.

"The cat. He's knocking more things off the shelves. Take a look."

The heavyset man studied him. "Nah. I don't care about none of that. I'm here to see you."

"Can I help you find a book?" Brody asked.

"What's that supposed to mean?" Columbo asked. "You being a jerk or somethin'?"

"This *is* a bookstore."

"No, it ain't."

"Then what is it?"

"You know what it is."

"A mystery bookstore?" Brody asked.

"It's a mystery, all right. It's a mystery why you're here."

"As I've told several people—"

"Yeah, yeah. I heard. You were in the Navy, and you bought a bookstore. Yada yada yada."

"I don't think you're supposed to use yada that way."

Columbo's lip curled. "I'll use it any way I see fit."

Brody lifted his hands in mock surrender. "You're the customer."

"There you go being a jerk again."

"You're not a customer?"

"No, you rat." Columbo's hand went toward his pocket.

Brody was too far away from the man to make a play for the gun. If he hid in one of the aisles of books, it would only be seconds before the mobster found him. He had only one chance, and he took it.

"Shhh," Brody said, bringing a finger to his lips.

Columbo froze, his hand stuck in his pocket, presumably around a gun.

Brody tapped his ear then made a circular signal in the air. The heavyset man didn't understand what he was trying to communicate.

"What are—?"

Brody hushed the man again and brought his finger back to his lips. He moved slowly toward the counter and lifted the telephone receiver. He pointed at the earpiece, then made the circular motion again.

Columbo understood then. He jerked his head a couple of times toward the rear of the store, indicating he wanted Brody to go out to the alley.

The big man shook his head then slowly hung up the phone.

They stared at each other in awkward silence for a moment until Brody said, "You're Frankie Columbo, right?"

The mobster's eyes lit up with anger.

"I met your wife a couple of days ago when she brought your daughter in for a book. You own the little Italian restaurant, right?"

Columbo removed his hand from his pocket.

"That's right," he said, his voice almost a whisper. "And I've seen you around with that girl from the grocery store. The pretty one. She looks... fragile."

Brody's face flattened. Now, they had both scored a point.

"I came by looking for an associate of mine," Columbo said. "Perhaps you've seen him?"

"Who is that?"

Columbo smirked. "Seriously?"

Brody shrugged and shook his head at the same time, feigning ignorance.

"He's a very stocky man, likes the weights."

"Oh, him. Yeah, he was here a couple of days ago."

"He didn't come by last night?"

"Not that I know of."

"I sent him for a book, and he never came home."

"And you thought he would still be here? He's that slow of a reader?"

Columbo's nose crinkled. "I had to start looking for him somewhere."

"The store closes at five," Brody said. "If your friend came by after that, the cat may have eaten him."

"The cat?"

"Like I said, he's a menace."

"You did say that."

Something fell in the back of the store.

"The cat?" Columbo asked.

"See for yourself. Just keep your fingers curled in. He's likely to nip one of them and drop you into Lake Massabesic."

"What's that?" Columbo asked.

"The lake, it's across the border into New Hampshire."

"I know where it's at, meathead, but no cat is gonna do that—nip off a finger. Even one that's a menace."

"If you say so, but I'm not going to test him."

The heavyset man rolled his eyes, which caused Brody to smile. The mobster then glanced around the store. "This shop. It seems like it fits the talents of a bookkeeper."

"Excuse me?"

"That's what you did before you came to town, right? You were a bookkeeper."

Brody stared at him, refusing to answer.

Columbo waved his hand around. "You keep care of books. You're a bookkeeper."

He didn't believe the smile on the mobster's face. It was thin and practiced and hid something cruel behind it. Up until recently, Brody had lived in a world full of those smiles.

The heavyset man absently picked at something in his teeth. "If you see my associate, make sure you send him home. *Safe.*"

Columbo headed toward the door. He turned around and said, "If he's not safe..." He patted the gun in his pocket. "You get my point."

Brody definitely understood the man's point.

The bell brightly chimed as Columbo left the store.

Chapter 29

Shortly before noon, Constable Emery Farnsworth arrived outside The Red Herring. He climbed off his bike and put the kickstand down, leaving the bicycle outside the large store window. He removed his bike helmet and hung it from the handlebars. Next, he ran his fingers several times through his short hair. He then rolled his shoulders, inhaled deeply, and slowly exhaled. When he turned to look inside the store, he noticed Brody watching him. He tapped the window several times and pointed at the big man.

Brody pointed to himself and said, "Me?" to the nearly empty store. Only the cat was inside, and he was currently curled up asleep on a shelf that was labeled *Discounted Titles*.

The bell sounded when Farnsworth walked in. He immediately reached up and grabbed the brass chime, stopping it from making any further sound.

"That will throw off my customer count," Brody said.

"What?"

"Two bells for entry. Two bells for an exit. Now the whole system will be thrown off."

The officer blinked several times as he tried to understand what Brody was saying.

The big man decided it was probably best not to mess with Emery for too long today. He let him off the hook by asking, "What can I do for you, Constable?"

"Where were you last night?" His demeanor had taken on a level of officiousness that their previous interactions had lacked.

"I was here."

"In the bookstore?" Emery asked.

"In my apartment."

"That's not what I heard."

"What did you hear?"

"The rumor around town is that you had dinnah with Daphne. At her place."

"Sure, I had dinner with her, but then I came home and spent the night reading."

"What are you reading?"

He held up *The Deep Blue Good-by*.

Emery smirked. "That's why she likes you, isn't it?"

"Because I read?"

"No," he said defensively and turned to scan the bookstore. His gaze paused on the slightly crooked display of Carrie Fenton's books. "What happened there?"

"What happened, where?"

"*There*," Emery said, pointing at the leaning cardboard display. "It's bent and taped up."

"I tripped over the cat and fell onto it."

The officer's eyes took in the rest of the lobby area. "Something else is different," he said, his foot tapping on the hardwood of the floor.

"I also moved some books around," Brody said. "I'm trying to make the place more my own.

"That must be it." Emery's attention returned to him. "So last night you were in your apartment? Nobody can vouch for your whereabouts then?"

"Are you accusing me of something?"

"A body drifted ashore this morning up in York Harbah."

"A body?"

"That's right. The man was identified as James De Luca. The same man you fought with outside this store."

"You think *I* did it?"

"Word is that you're a formah Navy SEAL. That means you *definitely* could have done it."

"I didn't, though," Brody lied.

Besides, had he been a Navy SEAL, he probably would have understood the tides better. He had driven thirty minutes north to the town of Ogunquit, where he tossed Jimmy the Pump into the ocean. Brody had naively hoped a shark would eat him. He was originally from Kansas City and later migrated to Phoenix. He'd never so much as put a foot on an ocean beach until he arrived in Maine. How was he supposed to know how the tides actually worked?

Unfortunately, luck wasn't on his side. The sharks hadn't eaten the weightlifter after the current pulled his body out to sea. In fact, James De Luca's body was returned to land only ten minutes from Pleasant Valley. It seemed not even the Atlantic Ocean could stand dealing with Jimmy the Pump.

At least Brody had been smart enough to drive inland to Sanford to dispose of the rug. He threw it into an open dumpster behind a grocery store. On his way back home, he tossed the knitting needles and the skein of yarn into a trash can belonging to a random North Berwick homeowner.

As he drove along State Route 4, he threw Jimmy the Pump's wallet into some random trees. He thought about keeping the $87 the weightlifter had in his wallet, but Brody thought that would feel wrong. In his old life, he would not have hesitated to claim the money. However, he was trying to be a better person. He hadn't killed the man for profit or club loyalty. He had taken De Luca's life to protect his own. Stealing the money would somehow cheapen that.

That didn't stop him from knowing that he needed to get rid of the body though. He couldn't go to Emery Farnsworth and say he killed Jimmy the Pump in self-defense. If he did that, everyone would soon learn he was in the Witness Protection Program.

"I don't know of anyone else he had problems with," Emery said.

"You're only looking at me because of Daphne."

"That's not true. I'm looking at you because it's my job."

"Then you're saying I should spend the night with Daphne next time, so I have an alibi?"

Emery's face reddened. "That's definitely *not* what I'm saying to do."

"I don't know. It sounds exactly like what you're telling me to do."

The constable struggled to contain his emotions. Finally, he pointed two fingers toward his own eyes then pointed them toward Brody. "I'm watching you."

Brody nodded. "I've officially been put on notice."

"You bet you have." Emery stalked toward the front door, yanking it open. The brass bell swung wildly. "You have most definitely been put on notice. I only have one person on my watchlist, and that, my friend, is you."

"Hey, Emery."

"What?" he barked.

"Since you just said I'm a Navy SEAL, should you be talking to me that way?"

He blanched. "I didn't mean to say—"

"Have a nice day, Constable."

Emery stared at the big man. Finally, he mumbled, "Thank you for your service," and hurried out to his bicycle.

Chapter 30

"*The Talented Mr. Ripley*," Chloe Columbo said.

Brody stood at the end of the aisles. He wasn't sure if the book was a mystery, a cozy, a thriller, a true crime, or a classic. Those were the handwritten descriptions that someone, presumably Alice Walker, had labeled each aisle.

"Who wrote the book?"

The teenager eyed Brody. "Really?"

He raised an eyebrow.

"You own a mystery bookstore. That's something you should know."

"I don't have to know everything," the big man said.

"You didn't know what a protagonist was."

"Why are you busting my chops, kid?"

Chloe moved toward the aisle labeled *Classics*. "It was written by Patricia Highsmith."

"Highsmith," Brody repeated. "Got it. Hey, that was nice of you to recommend some books for the old man."

"What?"

"The waiter from the restaurant? He came in and bought three books by Raymond Chandler. I thought you recommended them."

"Not me. I've never read Chandler. Besides, the waiter can barely speak English. I didn't think he read it."

"Oh."

"And I'm sorry if I'm busting your chops. I'm just trying to figure you out."

"Me? Why?"

Chloe ran a finger along the spines of some nearby books. "Because you were nice to me. I get why most guys are nice to *her*."

"Her being your stepmother?"

"It's obvious why guys like her."

"A little too obvious."

The teenager smiled at that as she continued her hunt for the book. "It's not in this aisle," she said. "Probably mystery."

He followed her into the nearby aisle.

"But you were nice to me and sort of ignored her."

"Can't people be nice to you for the sake of being nice?"

As her finger trailed along with the books, she stopped. There was a hole where some books should have been. "If it was going to be in this aisle," the teenager said, tapping the shelf, "this is where it should have been."

Brody bent down and grabbed a stack of books the cat had knocked over earlier. He had placed them on a lower shelf without consideration to their proper place. He lifted them and quickly read the titles. The third book was Highsmith's novel. He handed it to Chloe.

"Most men aren't nice," the girl said.

"Some men are."

"Those men are looking for something."

"What are they looking for?"

She tilted her head and batted her eyes.

"Besides that," Brody said.

"If they don't want that, they want something from my father."

"You know about your dad?"

"He's my *father*. And, yeah, I know about him. He's more interested in being a big shot in the outfit than being with me."

"I'm sorry, Chloe."

"Don't be," she said and flipped through the book in her hands. "I stopped worrying about him when I was ten. Now the only thing I care about is not ending up like him."

"You won't be anything like him."

She nodded with her eyes still on the book. "I know. In a couple years, I'm leaving. I'm going to get away."

"What are you going to do?"

Chloe looked around to make sure no one was listening. "You were in the Navy, right? That's what I'm going to do, too. I'm going to sign up and go far away. I'm never coming back. He won't ever be able to get at me if I'm on a ship."

He watched her for a moment before asking, "Has he hit you, Chloe?"

"I should go."

Brody stepped aside so she could move toward the counter.

"Chloe, has he hurt you?"

She turned to stare at him. "It's not like that, but if I tell you, it'll sound stupid."

He softly smiled. "It won't sound stupid, I promise. I never met my dad, and my mom was an addict. She hated me and took every chance she had to tell me so.”

“At least she talked to you.”

Brody’s smile faded.

“My father ignores me. He’s never told me he loves me.”

“I’m sorry.”

“I’m here because a judge mandated it. I tried to stop seeing my father, but he pressured my mom. He doesn’t even pay child support. Not that he has to. No, he forced her to agree that she gets nothing. He’s a horrible man.”

Travis ambled out then and rubbed against Chloe’s leg. Tears welled in her eyes.

“I can’t wait for the day when I walk out of his life and never look back.”

Brody slowly put an arm around the girl. She leaned into him and cried. For several moments, they remained silent.

“It’s okay,” he finally said. “You can hang out here as long as you want.”

Chloe moved away from him and wiped her eyes with a balled fist. “I wish I could, but we’re leaving once I get done here.”

“Leaving?”

“We’re going back to Boston, which is cool. At least, I’ll be home with my mom.”

“Everything will be okay then?”

“As okay as it can be.” She handed him the book.

“No,” he said. “That’s yours. A gift from Travis and me.”

She clutched the book to her chest, and the tears started again.

Brody gave her a quick hug then leaned back to see her better. "This is your last chance to take the cat with you," he said. "You could always leave him with your father."

"My father would hate him."

"Which is why you should take him."

Chloe laughed.

Chapter 31

A roar pierced the quiet of the store. It was a raspy growl that Brody knew intimately.

He dropped the books he'd picked up from another of the cat's messes and ran toward the front window.

It was a beautiful two-seater chopper. The custom ride was initially built in the 1970s by one of the founding members of the Satan's Dawgs. A few years ago, it had been rebuilt to restore it to its original glory. A soft-tail frame with ape-hanger bars, it featured a Sportster tank painted black and adorned with an angry, barking dog with devil horns sprouting from its head.

The bike had been his when he was the bookkeeper for the club. Now, Suicide Mike Eslick rode it as if the beauty belonged to him. Mike was designated the club's dogcatcher. He was the man given the unenviable task of watching the club's members for any acts of disloyalty or treason. For some reason, the man relished it. The cops had Internal Affairs. The Satan's Dawgs had their dogcatcher.

As the chopper stopped at the intersection near his store, Brody felt hate welling up inside him. Not only was Suicide Mike a big reason he was able to be turned by the FBI, but the man was also now riding his bike. He looked at his hands. They weren't shaking like before when the corporate puke drove through on his shiny Fat Boy.

No, hate was a feeling Brody knew well, and it warmed him like a blanket on a cold morning.

Suicide Mike was an ugly man, earning his moniker from ramming his first motorcycle into the side of a Honda Civic while running from the cops. When asked why he did it, Mike told the police he'd rather be dead than in handcuffs. The legend stuck, and his moniker was born.

Eslick didn't wear a helmet, choosing only a pair of leather aviator goggles. His long, dirty hair and scraggly beard jarred with the peaceful nature of the community. Onderdonk was right for making Brody cut his off. The biker stuck out like a teenager's first zit.

Suicide Mike turned his attention toward The Red Herring, which caused Brody to jump away from the window. He heard his old bike rev several times.

When he peeked out again, Mike was rolling down Main Street. The rider pointed to the left and turned onto Second Avenue, where Il Cuoco Irato was. One thought came to Brody immediately.

Suicide Mike is meeting with Frankie the Dove.

Brody burst through the front door and ran down Main Street. Several people on the sidewalk hurried out of his way. In front of Pleasant Valley Sundae, though, a group of children wandered out from the store. To avoid them, the big man hopped into the street without looking.

A passing Audi angrily honked its horn right before it hit him.

His feet left the ground, and he went spiraling to the pavement.

He rolled several times before coming to a stop. He stood as fast as he could, desperately trying to get his bearings. Woozy from the collision, he stepped back onto the sidewalk. The driver, a middle-aged woman, stared at him with horror, her hands covering her mouth.

Brody waved apologetically to her and was about to turn and run when the children surrounded him, full of questions.

A kid with a flattop haircut tugged on his khakis. "Did you break your noggin?"

"You got hit by a car, mister," a second kid said, stating the obvious.

Another roar came from up the street. Brody's head whipped in that direction, causing his world to tilt suddenly. To stabilize himself, he reached out and put his hand on the head of Captain Obvious.

"Are you going to fall down, mister?" a little girl with pigtails asked. She held a melting ice cream cone in her hand.

"Are you going to barf?" the kid under Brody's hand asked.

Two motorcycles, their engines loudly growling, slowly made their way along Main Street.

The kid with the flattop tugged on Brody's pants and said, "You should call your mom."

Brody looked down to see chocolate ice cream smeared on his khakis.

The two bikes continued to crawl toward him. He couldn't go back toward his store because he would come face-to-face with the riders. If he ran down Main Street, they would see him running.

He had only one choice.

Brody let go of the kid's head and stepped inside the ice cream shop.

The noise was unbearable as the children screamed and laughed. From a set of speakers hanging in the corner of the store, 1950s Rockabilly music played cheerfully loud.

A single father was leaned over, his head in one hand while the other fiddled with his cell phone. Several hapless mothers looked his way. Brody couldn't tell if the women were silently begging him for help or if they wanted him to take their children away. Either way, he wasn't their man.

A kid ran by him, dragging a sticky hand across the knee of his khakis, leaving a mark of melted green ice cream. The kid giggled and ran away.

The big man stepped further into the store.

"Can I help you, sir?" the teenager behind the counter asked.

Brody eyed her for a moment before looking at the ice cream in the chilled counter. "I haven't decided yet."

She sighed and rolled her eyes. "Take your time."

Two kids ran by him this time, each smacking their hands onto his pants. A couple of mothers yelled, "Hey!" at them, but neither moved to corral the vermin they had birthed. Brody scowled at the women. Both apologetically shrugged as if there was nothing they could do.

He turned to the window as two riders he recognized passed by. The red-haired man was nicknamed Chester after the Cheetos mascot, and the balding man with the long hair was called Skullet. They both rode Sportsters and wore leather vests known as cuts. Neither had a Satan's Dawgs patch on the back.

In club vernacular, they were pups—club prospects, not full members. Brody knew their purpose for being in town. They were additional muscle for Suicide Mike.

The group of laughing and screaming kids circling him had grown, each smacking his khaki pants.

Now, four parents were yelling various forms of "Stop it!" to children with names like Aidan, Isabella, Kaylee, and Landon. Again, the adults all remained in their seats, not moving to aid Brody with their hellspawn.

He growled at the children. They paused momentarily; their eyes wide with fear. That made him happy. Finally, someone had shown the children what real authority and respect was.

Then one of the kids squealed with delight, and the game of smearing his pants with ice cream began again.

Several of the parents yelled, "No!" in unison.

Brody grunted something that was the closest thing to an expletive he would allow and headed for the door.

"I guess you don't want any ice cream," the teenager said from behind the counter. "Whatever."

Chapter 32

The ringing of the bell annoyed him as he re-entered the store.

I need to remove that stupid thing, he thought angrily.

Then she popped out from the *Cozy* aisle, and the ringing of the bell no longer bothered him.

"You're back!" Daphne Winterbourne said. She held a paperback in her hand. "I was wondering where you were." Her words trailed off as she saw the ice cream smears around his khaki pants. "What happened to you?" she asked with a cringe.

"The ice cream store threw up on me."

She scrunched her nose.

"What are you doing here?" Brody asked.

"What do you think?" she said, holding up a paperback copy of Jim Thompson's *The Grifters*. "Besides, I wanted to say how much fun I had last night. I hope we can do it again."

For the briefest of seconds, the big man let himself think about their dinner together.

"Would you like to come over tonight? Nothing fancy, but after we eat, maybe we could go for a walk."

"I'd love to," Brody said as he stepped toward the window. He could see the two prospects now heading up the street toward the bookstore. As they walked, people moved away from them. No one appeared to be smiling at the men. "But we need to go."

"What do you mean?

"Now!" Brody yelled, grabbing her by the hand.

"Where are we going? I only have a few minutes for my break."

He hurried toward the back of the store, pulling Daphne behind him.

"What's going on?" she asked.

"We can't stay here."

"I don't understand. Tell me what's happening."

Once they were in the alley, he held her hands. "Go back to the grocery store. I'll come get you in a bit and explain everything."

She stared at him, confused.

He kissed her on the forehead. "Please, Daphne."

"Tell me what's going on, Brody."

"I can't. Not right now. You need to go. Now! Please, trust me."

She stepped out of the alley and began the walk back to The Pleasant Peasant.

Brody trailed behind, his eyes warily watching the two thugs who had crossed the street as they moved toward his store. Several times he caught Daphne looking back at him. Each time, he shooed her on. He couldn't do what was needed with her around.

When she was out of sight, he trotted up the block to Main Street and saw them entering his store. Brody confidently walked toward The Red

Herring, pushed the door slightly open, and grabbed the brass bell before it could ring.

"He's not here," Chester muttered.

Skullet turned to see Brody holding the brass bell.

"Hey, fellas," he said, closing the door and locking it. He flipped the *Open* sign to *Closed*.

Chester turned to his partner with wide eyes. "It's him."

Skullet nodded knowingly. It was clear who was the brains of the team. They both slowly turned to the big man.

"You boys looking to earn your patches?"

Skullet's lip curled. "If we bring you in, we're sure to get our colors."

"Then get to earning," Brody said. He grabbed a book from the Carrie Fenton display and threw it at Chester, causing the man to duck.

The balding prospect removed a knife from his belt and flicked it open. He sliced the air toward the big man, missing him. Skullet took two small hops toward Brody, stabbing the air each time like a sword fighter in a swashbuckler movie.

Brody grabbed the entire Carrie Fenton cardboard display and repeatedly hit his opponent with it, swinging it back and forth, sending books flying about the store. It wasn't meant to cause pain but merely be a nuisance or distraction while Brody figured out his next move. The bottom of the display caught the end of the knife. It clattered to the hardwood floor.

He threw the cardboard display after the weapon. The prospect's eyes darted around the shop looking for his blade.

Chester took that as his opportunity to attack Brody, but he was a clumsy fighter. His punches were roundhouses, like the type seen in bad B movies. Brody's jabs, however, snapped with ferocity. He wasn't just angry—he was focused on defending his new life, Daphne, even the darn cat. No lousy prospects were going to take this away from him.

His punches hit the red-haired man in the face, once, then twice, exploding his nose. Blood cascaded down his lips and chin. Chester covered his face with his hands.

Skullet found his knife and returned to the fight, poking at the bigger man and working to find his range.

Brody knew he had to do something fast. He'd already pressed his luck for too long. Fighting a man with a blade was a losing proposition. He grabbed the nearest hardback book from a shelf. As Skullet reached out, Brody smacked the prospect's wrist with the book's spine.

The balding man yelped and yanked his hand back.

Brody stepped forward, but the prospect lashed out again with his knife. He winced in pain as he did so. The two men stared at each other for a moment, and then Skullet worked up the courage to stab again. Brody smacked him once more on the wrist with the spine of the hardback book.

The blade clattered to the floor amid another cry of pain from the prospect.

Brody didn't waste time. He moved forward, striking Skullet alongside the head with the flat of the hardback book. He reversed the strike and hit him on the opposite side of the face. When Skullet collapsed to the floor on his back, Brody straddled him and struck him twice with the spine of the book, driving it down like a guillotine.

He was about to hit him a third time when it occurred to him that he didn't have to kill the man. In fact, he didn't want to kill him. His new life in Pleasant Valley had put a lot of odd thoughts into his head, and not killing an adversary was about the strangest.

Skullet struggled to breathe, but the man was alive. He was a bloody mess, but he was still among the living.

Brody relaxed and lowered his hands. He took a moment to read the title of the blood-spattered book he held. It was *Murder, She Wrote: Murder in Red* by Jessica Fletcher and Jon Land.

Something dragged against the wood floor, and Brody quickly glanced back to see Chester picking up the knife. The other prospect stepped toward him, slashing the blade awkwardly in the air as he moved. It was clear the man had not fought with a knife before.

Brody rolled off the unconscious man, jumped up, and stood at the ready. Blood dripped from the book in his hand.

The biker lifted the knife above his head and yelled a guttural sound that made little sense. His hand came down with speed and fury, like every villain in a slasher film. It was an inept attack and one that Brody avoided. He redirected Chester's hand back into the man's thigh. The biker squeaked once in pain and stumbled awkwardly away.

Both men stared at the knife protruding from Chester's leg. Blood slowly spread out from the wound.

"Looks like that hurts," Brody said.

"I should go to a hospital," the prospect muttered.

He shrugged. "You're probably fine."

Then Brody thrashed Chester about the head and shoulders with the spine of the hardback book, spraying drops of blood throughout The Red Herring, Pleasant Valley's only shop catering to tales of crime and mystery.

Chapter 33

It was a hasty job of cleaning up the store.

One at a time, he carried both unconscious men into the basement and locked the door from the outside. Not killing the two prospects felt like he made a positive change in his life, but it did create a set of problems.

What should he do with them now?

How long would they remain unconscious?

Chester had a severe wound that didn't appear life-threatening, but Brody wasn't a doctor.

If he did nothing and the prospect died from his wound, was he responsible?

Should I call for help? he wondered.

The questions plagued Brody as he ran up to his apartment. He hurriedly changed his shirt and pants as they were covered with both blood and ice cream. In new attire, he returned to the bookstore.

He was about to formulate a plan of action when he saw the older man outside the store. With hands around his eyes, Herbert Paxton pressed his face against the window of the front door. When he saw the big man inside, he knocked several times.

"I'm closed," Brody yelled.

The older man pounded once again.

"Closed!" Brody hollered and waved him on.

Herb frowned and changed his tactic. He tapped his knuckles against the door in a steady rhythm that quickly became annoying.

"Persistent old coot," Brody muttered and hurried to the door. He unlocked it and pulled it open.

"What are you doing?" Herb asked.

"Nothing," Brody said. Quickly realizing that it was an inadequate response, he followed it up with, "Getting ready to get some lunch."

"You're not going to sell many books if you close down in the middle of the day."

"I'm doing fine as it is."

Herb's eyes scanned the store. "Geez Louise, what happened in here?"

"The cat's helping me remodel."

The older man pushed past Brody. His eyes first went to the destroyed cardboard display, then the tipped-over book spinner.

"Bulldog did all this?"

"Bulldog?"

"Bulldog Drummond. My name for the cat."

Herb bent down and touched his fingers to the hardwood floor. When he lifted them, he rubbed them together. "That's blood, boy."

"It is?" Brody asked.

"You sure Bulldog is okay?"

"He's fine. That was from me. I got a bloody nose from the cat."

"The cat gave you a bloody nose?"

"He bonked me."

Herb studied Brody's face. "There's blood all ovah your head and neck, boy."

Brody swallowed. He hadn't bothered to check himself in a mirror while in his apartment.

The older man's eyes narrowed as he continued to examine Brody's nose. "Must have been a heck of a bleedah."

"He was."

"What?"

"It was. My nose, I mean."

"Where's the cat?" Herb slowly asked. "Hey, Bulldog, where you at?"

The older man walked into the middle of the store. He placed his hands on his hips. "I like that cat. You better hope nothing has happened to him."

"Him? I'm the one with the bloody nose."

"You probably deserved it," the old man said with a decisive nod.

Travis wandered out then, looked up at Herb, and sat. The old man said, "That's what I like about cats. They only need to see you. Don't need a whole lot of love beyond that."

"Was there something you wanted, Herb? I've really got to get going."

"Geez, some people have got no patience. I was coming by to tell you something about Alice, but if you ain't got time to hear it..."

Brody held up his hands. "What is it?"

"Remember I said there was something she was working on with that writah girl?"

"Yeah," Brody said. "I already talked with her."

"Carrie told you about their story?"

Brody was surprised Herb would know about Carrie writing Alice's biography. That would reveal too much about Alice's life as Evelyn Spier and would jeopardize her position in the Witness Protection Program. He thought she would have been more careful in her life.

"She told me she was writing a book," Brody said. "She didn't say what it was about."

"See, Navy boy," the old man said, smiling. "I know something you don't."

"Herb, just tell me what you know so you can leave me in peace."

"They were working on a heist story, wiseacre."

"A heist?"

"You know, a robbery."

"I know what a heist is."

"It was pretty exciting how Alice and Carrie laid it out."

"Why would they tell you?"

"The two of them needed my advice."

"Your advice?"

"Ayuh, I used to be a city plannah for a lot of years. I know the ins and outs of all the buildings in Pleasant Valley."

"Were they asking you about a specific building?"

"That's right. They were asking about the building where the little Italian restaurant is now. Had a whole story planned for it."

Brody shook his head then. He knew what the two women had been doing and suddenly believed Alice Walker was very much alive.

Chapter 34

Brody quickly walked down Main Street toward The Pleasant Peasant. Several people smiled and nodded at him as he hurried. He did his best to be polite, but he was in a rush, and his head swiveled back and forth, searching for Suicide Mike Eslick or Frankie the Dove.

After finishing his conversation with Herb, he washed his face in the bookstore's restroom. Then he left voicemails for both U.S. Marshal Ted Onderdonk and FBI Special Agent Max Ekleberry. Brody wasn't sure what he would tell the men when he talked with them, but he realized he needed their help.

Would he tell them about the two Satan Dawg's prospects? Beating them and locking them in the basement was an abnormal reaction for Bookkeeper Beau Smith, but not calling the cops for help felt quite reasonable.

And what about Jimmy the Pump? Should he tell the lawmen about his demise? He killed the man in self-defense but dumping his body in the ocean and scattering various pieces of evidence around the Maine countryside was suspect. Those weren't the actions of an innocent man.

Another thought entered his mind. The Dawgs knew he was in Pleasant Valley because the mob was onto him.

Brody slowed his walk.

How? he wondered. *How did the mob get onto me?*

At first, he thought it was because they had discovered Alice. If she was alive, maybe they hadn't recognized her. Then how did they find him?

Would they have seen his picture on the FBI Rats website without seeing Alice's? Was that possible? It was not possible, Brody finally decided. It was highly unlikely.

Therefore, they had found her before his arrival. That meant when she disappeared and he showed up, they would have already assumed the bookstore was a U.S. Marshal cover. They would have made him from the get-go. Using the FBI Rats website would have made it easy for them to put the pieces together and discover who he was.

So maybe Alice discovered the mob was onto her and she figured she had to slip out of town. If that were the case, she would have told U.S. Marshal Onderdonk. Instead, she disappeared.

And he thought he knew why.

He was lost in thought as he arrived at the grocery store.

The same sickening Muzak was playing as before, and the irritatingly bright lights shone down on the shiny tiled floors. A crowd of people gathered at the front of the store.

Brody approached the group which had formed a semi-circle around the cashier, Aaron, who was sitting on the ground. His nose was bleeding, and he held a hand over his left eye.

"What happened?" Brody asked.

The crowd of workers and shoppers parted when he spoke. They all seemed to relax now that someone was there asking appropriate questions.

"A couple men came in," Aaron said, "and they took Daphne." He was no longer snotty toward Brody.

"What did these men look like?"

"One of them looked like a real hoodlum. A motorcycle type. He was smelly, too."

"And the other one? Was he a fat guy in a tracksuit? The owner of Il Cuoco Irato?"

Aaron's one open eye peered at him like he'd lost his mind. "No. He was a handsome type, dressed in slacks and a club shirt."

"Tall and thin?" Brody asked.

Aaron nodded with his right hand still pressed to his eye.

"Did he whistle while he walked?"

"He sure did. He punched me in the eye then whistled as he left the store."

A siren wailed from outside. The crowd turned to watch Constable Emery Farnsworth's bicycle skid to a stop in front of the building.

"Wait here," Brody said to the group. Nobody thought about challenging his order.

He walked outside and met Emery as he dismounted his bike and switched off the siren. The officer eyed him with contempt.

"How am I not surprised to find you here?" Emery said.

"A couple of guys grabbed Daphne," Brody said.

The officer froze. "What?"

"You've got a mob operation in town. The Italian restaurant."

"That's not true," Farnsworth said, "and that's dangerously close to profiling."

"They're laundering money through the restaurant. I don't know how, but they are."

"Laundering money? Is that why they took Daphne? Do they need a bookkeepah?"

"They took her because of me."

Emery's lip curled. "What did you do?"

Brody had already lied about being a naval officer and a SEAL, so he figured another wouldn't hurt at this moment. He lowered his voice. "I'm an FBI agent."

"You're with the FBI?" The officer's eyes swept over Brody. "Show me your badge."

"I'm undercover. I don't have it with me."

"Right."

"Don't be an idiot, Emery. That's why James De Luca attacked me. He found out I was an agent."

"Is that why you killed him?"

"Stop it," Brody said. "I would imagine his boss wasn't happy he brought attention to their operation by fighting with me. I bet he killed him because he got sloppy."

"That's a convenient story."

"Sometimes life is convenient," Brody said.

Emery's face scrunched. "What does that mean?"

"It means the mob knows I'm watching them, and they know I'm seeing Daphne."

"So they take Daphne to make you, what, go away? That doesn't make sense."

"They grab her to make me come to them."

"Oh."

"I need some back-up. Will you help me?"

"Help... you?"

"Yes, Emery. I need *your* help. The FBI needs *your* help."

When the understanding that the Federal Bureau of Investigation needed his help dawned on Constable Emery Farnsworth, he slowly smiled, and his eyes widened.

"Let's go," Brody said.

They ran to Second Avenue and rounded the corner. Il Cuoco Irato sat in a few buildings. Suicide Mike's motorcycle, Brody's former ride, was brazenly parked in front of the little restaurant.

"Wait here," Brody said.

"I should go with you," Emery said. "You don't even have a gun."

"Then let me have yours."

The officer put his hand on his weapon. "Then I won't have one."

Brody stared at him for a moment. "Fine. Keep it but call for help."

"The chief is still out of town."

"Then call the national guard, Emery. I don't care who you get, just get someone. There's a lot more trouble coming, Constable. More trouble than you and I can handle."

Brody stepped off the curb and jogged toward the little restaurant. He opened the door but stopped immediately to take in the scene.

Francis "Frankie the Dove" Columbo was next to the old waiter, both with their hands in the air.

Near the entrance, two masked robbers stood with guns drawn.

From the little hanging speakers, Dean Martin sang, "Ain't That a Kick in the Head."

One of the robbers turned to Brody, shoved a revolver into the big man's face, and said, "Get your hands in the air!"

Chapter 35

Brody studied the robbers. They were considerably smaller than him, and black balaclavas covered their heads down to their necks. They both wore loose-fitting jackets even though it was mid-summer.

"Get your hands in the air!" the robber repeated, trying desperately to disguise her voice as a male's. It didn't work.

Brody slowly lifted his hands as he turned his attention to Frankie the Dove and the old waiter.

"Where's the money?" the other robber yelled. She also tried to disguise her voice low like a male. It wasn't any better than the first.

"I don't know what you're talking about," the Dove said.

"Where's the money?" the smaller of the two robbers said. "We know another shipment came in on a boat a couple of nights ago."

Columbo's brow furrowed. "And how would you know that?"

The two robbers glanced at each other.

His eyes widening, the elderly waiter glanced toward Frankie the Dove. The older man took a small step back.

"Why are you bringing cash through the bay?" Brody asked.

Columbo's lip curled. "You think I'm just gonna spill my plans to you? Do I look like a villain in a James Bond movie?"

"Wouldn't it have been easier to bring it up the interstate?"

"Wouldn't it have been easier…" the Dove said in a mocking tone. "I'm not telling you squat, but you've all told me everything I need to know. I've gotta snitch in my organization."

"Where's the money?" the smaller one asked again, lifting her gun higher in emphasis.

"Somebody's talking," the mobster said, lowering his hands until they were on his hips. "When I find who, they're dead. Just like the lot of you."

"What did you do with Daphne?" Brody asked.

"Keep your mouth shut, rat," Frankie the Dove said, "while I deal with these two."

"Daphne?" the smaller of the robbers said. Her voice sounded genuinely feminine for the first time. "He did something to Daphne?"

Brody looked at the robber. He couldn't make out any details due to the balaclava and the over-sized coat. They were good choices in selecting a disguise. "He took her because he'd seen us together."

The robber turned back at Columbo. "What did you do with Daphne Winterbourne?" she asked.

Frankie the Dove's eyes narrowed. "What do you know about that broad?"

"I know if you don't tell me, I'm going to shoot you."

"You won't shoot me," Columbo said.

"But I will," Brody said. "And you know that's the truth."

"You don't even have a gun, so stay out of this, bookkeepah."

The smaller robber looked at him. "You're the new owner of The Red Herring?"

"Yeah."

"You know Ted Onderdonk?" she whispered.

"He's on the way, Alice."

"Alice Walkah?" Columbo said. "We wondered where you went. Just when we were ready to grab you, you disappeared."

The other robber put her hand on Alice's shoulder. "We should get out of here."

"You're here now, Carrie," Brody said. "See it through."

Carrie Fenton repeatedly blinked behind her balaclava.

"Not only did that snitch tell you about the money coming in, but he must've told you about our plans to grab you. Who's the rat in my crew?"

"You knew about Alice?" Brody asked Columbo.

"Of course, we knew about Alice. Or should I say, *Evelyn Spier*? My friends have been looking for her for a long time. You got some dues to pay in the Windy City."

Alice Walker handed Brody her gun. When he took it from her, Frankie the Dove's hands immediately went into the air.

"Hey now," the heavyset man said, "can we talk about this like gentlemen?"

Brody pointed the gun at Frankie the Dove.

Alice gently put her hand on Brody's wrist. "Do me a favor, hon."

"What's that?"

"Don't shoot the waiter. He's with me."

Everyone looked at the older man who took another step away from the mobster.

"You!" Columbo exclaimed. "I trusted you. I brought you from the old country, and you treat me like this."

"Frankie!" Brody hollered.

"*What?*" he yelled, irritated by the interruption.

"You've got one chance to tell me where she is. Any answer other than where she is will get you shot."

"Why should I—"

The noise was deafening in the small restaurant. The older man next to Columbo flinched as the heavyset man fell to the floor, clutching his knee.

Carrie yelled at Brody, "What did you do?"

Alice pulled her partner back. "Let the man work."

Columbo writhed on the floor, clutching his leg.

Brody walked up to the mobster and pointed the gun at him. He lifted his eyes to the old Italian first and asked, "I'm guessing you speak English?"

"Enough," he said in a heavy Italian accent.

"Do you know where the money is?" Brody asked the waiter.

"I tried to find out where they hid it, but no luck."

"You should join them."

The waiter hurried back to where the two women waited. Alice had pulled off her mask. Carrie Fenton still wore hers.

"You're dead!" Columbo yelled from the ground. "All of you!"

Carrie Fenton stood near the window, peeking outside. "There's a cop out there!" she shouted. "He's hiding behind a tree."

"That's the local constable."

"Emery?" Alice said.

"He's with me. Make sure he stays there. If he moves, yell."

"He's on the phone," Carrie said. "He must have heard the gunshot."

Alice suddenly appeared at Brody's side, eyeing him. "You look like you've done this type of thing before. How do we get out of this?"

"I'm gonna kill you all!" the mobster yelled. "I'm gonna kill you and your families!"

"Step back, Alice," Brody said, his voice calm and reassuring. "This is about to get bloody."

Chapter 36

When Brody exited the building, he walked past his motorcycle and ran his hand over the ape-hanger handlebars. Constable Emery Farnsworth stepped from behind a tree and yelled, "Freeze!"

His feet were shoulder-width apart, and he stood crouched, his arms in a V-shape as his hands cupped his revolver. It was a classic patrol officer stance. What wasn't classic was the bike helmet tipped back on his head, the bicycle shorts, and the running shoes.

Brody didn't freeze. Instead, he strode toward the officer.

"Put it down," Brody ordered.

Emery looked at the weapon in Brody's hand and the blood that covered his khakis. "I'm not sure if I should lower my gun," the constable said.

"I'm not going to shoot you, Emery. Besides, if I wanted to do so, I would have done it by now." Brody turned the gun he carried backward and offered it to the constable.

Emery slowly lowered his pistol but didn't take the gun Brody had offered. "Where's Daphne?"

"She wasn't there."

"I heard two shots."

"There's a mob boss in there."

"Is he...?"

"Dead? Yeah."

"Crud!" Emery said and stepped off the sidewalk toward the restaurant. "Oh man, this is bad!"

"Emery!"

The constable turned to Brody. "What!"

"You don't need to go in there. The man is dead. He'll keep until we get back. I know where Daphne is, and we need to get her. Now."

Emery nodded and stepped back onto the sidewalk. "Where is she?"

"They've taken her to her house. They want to capture me there."

"Capture you? Why?"

So Suicide Mike can take me back to the club and put me down for all to see.

But Brody couldn't tell the officer that. So, he said, "They want to torture an FBI agent."

"You can't go there," Emery said.

"I have to. We have to. Were you able to get help?"

"Yes," he said. "The state patrol is on the way."

"The state patrol?"

Farnsworth nodded.

"Great," Brody said. "They'll be able to write some traffic tickets when they get here."

***

As they hurried, Brody recalled what had just occurred inside Il Cuoco Irato. It took some physical pressure to get Frankie the Dove to give him what he needed. Eventually, the mobster told him about Suicide Mike and another man he referred to as the Fixer. The two men concocted the plan to take Daphne to her house.

Brody knew why they were doing it. They believed they could set an ambush. Well, that was fine with him. Brody had lived through a couple of traps before. He had every intention of living through another.

For a moment, he thought about letting the mobster live. He didn't want to kill Chloe's father, even if he was the biggest jerk in the world to her. Maybe the guy would have a moment of clarity wherein he would realize he had missed an opportunity to love his daughter. If he killed Columbo, there would never be a chance for that moment of healing.

But then Frankie the Dove had to seal his fate by saying, "I will hunt you down, bookkeepah. If it's my last breath, you will nevah be free from me. And I'll kill that grocery girl, too. You can count on that."

He knew those words were valid. The anger and hatred Francis Columbo felt would never diminish. He'd just shot the man in the knee, for crying out loud, and tortured him to find out where Daphne was. Frankie the Dove wasn't the type of person to forgive and forget. Therefore, Brody had only one option.

He already thought he would like to stop by What's the Point? and purchase a new knitting kit. He'd only just cleared the book on Columbo,

and he was feeling the stress. He still had two
entries left to make.

Suicide Mike and some heavy named the
Fixer.

***

They were at the end of Daphne's block. In
the afternoon sun, the neighborhood looked
peaceful and charming.

Brody inhaled deeply, smelling the ocean's
aroma. The humidity had stuck his shirt to his
back. He'd only been in Pleasant Valley a few
days, and he'd already fallen in love with this
little town.

Because of today's events, he knew his time
here was now limited. Once he saved Daphne,
there would be no turning back. Everyone
would know his story. He wouldn't be able to
keep his secret much longer.

"What's the plan?" Emery asked, carefully
placing his hand on Brody's shoulder. His
attention was focused on Daphne's house.

The big man eyed the constable. Even though
he was an officer of the law, Brody sort of liked
the goofy fellow. Pretending to be a citizen was
messing with the former bookkeeper's
sensibilities.

"Why don't you go around back?" Brody
suggested.

"The back?"

"Cover the rear of the house, in case someone
comes out running."

"But that means you'll go in alone."

"I'll cover the back if you want to go inside alone. There's only two of us, Emery, and we need to handle it like professionals."

The officer patted his shoulder. "You're the FBI. You've been trained for this. If you think I should take the back of the house, well, mistah, I'll take the back. Call me a team playah."

The constable jogged into the nearest yard and moved to the rear of the house. Brody waited until Emery disappeared from view.

Then he began the walk toward Daphne's house. He thought about slinking toward the front door or maybe crouching into a run. Everything about it seemed wrong. No matter how he approached the house, they would see him. It was broad daylight. In Pleasant Valley, Maine no less.

He didn't want a shootout on Blue Street. This town shouldn't be subjected to the continuing drama of the Satan's Dawgs or the mob.

So, he did the only thing possible. He tucked his gun into his waistband and walked with his head up, and his shoulders pulled back. If Suicide Mike or the Fixer wanted to shoot him, then he would take his punishment like a man. He wouldn't back away from it. He was betting Mike wanted to take him alive, though.

When he reached the white picket fence at Daphne's house, no shot rang out. He opened the gate, took a moment to touch a purple flower, then proceeded up the sidewalk to the front porch. As he ascended the stairs, he prepared himself for a bullet to rip through his flesh.

His footsteps sounded heavy on the wooden porch. His fist banged on the door, causing it to swing slightly open.

"Come on in, Beau," Suicide Mike Eslick said. "We've been waiting for you."

Chapter 37

Daphne sat duct-taped to a dining room chair. A piece of thick silver tape covered her mouth, and she stared at him, her eyes wide with fear and confusion. Suicide Mike stood behind her with his hand on her shoulder.

"Pull out your gun—carefully—and kick it over here," the tall thin man in the corner said. He was impeccably dressed. He wore a black club shirt, olive drab slacks, and expensive-looking loafers. His dark hair was cut short on the sides but remained thick on the top.

Slowly, Brody removed his gun from the back of his pants. He laid the pistol on the ground and kicked it over to the impeccably dressed man. When he stood upright, he took a step toward the end table where the ceramic rhinoceros proudly stood.

"Been a long time, brother," Mike said.

The big man shook his head. "We're not brothers."

"We're brothers until the council says we're not."

Brody knew better than to argue further. Once a Dawg in the club, the only way out was death or ex-communication. Death was an easier way. If he returned to the club, the ex-communication ceremony was an ugly and painful process. It was that way, so members would never consider leaving.

The tall man began to whistle softly.

"You must be the Fixer," Brody said.

"And you must be the rat."

Suicide Mike chuckled.

"What do we do now?" Brody asked, his eyes focused on Daphne's.

"We wait," Mike said, his hand absently twirling Daphne's hair.

"Wait?" Brody asked.

"The Dawgs are on the way."

Brody's heart began to race. "Which Dawgs?"

Mike's grin was malicious. "The entire club, man. There's never been a rat like you, Beau. The whole crew has some pent-up aggression. They're going to love tearing this place apart."

"They don't need to come here. This is a nice town."

Mike sneered at him. "This place has made you soft, Beau. I can't believe you chose to live here."

"I didn't choose it."

"Yeah? Who did?"

Brody didn't answer.

"The marshals picked it for you, didn't they?"

The Fixer pointed his gun at Brody. "Answer him."

"Yeah, they picked it."

Suicide Mike leaned down to Daphne's ear. "See? I told you he was a rat."

Daphne stared at Brody with tears in her eyes.

"This man was a stone-cold killer, princess. Then he rolled on us to save his own skin."

Suicide Mike kissed Daphne's cheek. "You love a rat. It sounds like a Disney movie."

Brody eyed the two gunmen. The first thing he needed to do was get Daphne safe, but he only had a few cards to play. Now was the time to begin laying them on the table.

"I've alerted the FBI and the U.S. Marshals about you being here, Mike."

The biker raised his eyebrows and looked to the Fixer, who shrugged in return.

"State patrol is on the way, too," Brody said.

That got a laugh from both men.

"The staties?" Mike said. "What about the boy scouts? You call them, too?"

"There's a cop out back."

Their laughing stopped.

"There better not be," Mike said.

"He's the local constable."

"Constable?" Mike uttered.

Daphne muttered something into the tape covering her mouth.

Suicide Mike bent down to Daphne's ear. "You know this cop?"

She nodded.

The Fixer said, "I'll take a look," and moved toward the back of the house.

Mike and Brody stared at each other.

"Thanks for bringing my bike," Brody said.

"You ain't getting it back, Beau."

"Oh, she's coming back to me."

"There *is* a cop outside," the Fixer yelled.

When Mike turned his head to respond, Brody took another half step toward the end table.

"Deal with him," the biker yelled.

"You deal with him," the Fixer called back.

Mike turned and eyed Brody for a moment. Then he moved away from Daphne to look down the hallway. "What's he doing?" Mike asked.

Brody bent slightly at his knees and picked up the ceramic rhinoceros. He cupped it in his hand, hiding the weighty statue behind his arm.

Daphne's eyes widened, and Brody winked at her.

"He's talking to someone on his cell phone," the Fixer hollered.

Mike turned back to Brody. "Who's he talking to?"

"The state patrol," he said. "I already told you."

The biker turned his attention toward the hall and yelled, "He's talking to the state—"

Brody threw the ceramic statue then.

Suicide Mike noticed the motion in his peripheral vision and ducked out of the way. Unfortunately for him, he moved right into the path of the flying rhinoceros. The heavy knickknack hit him squarely in the temple, and its ceramic horn pierced his skull.

The biker's knees buckled, and his eyes fluttered in surprise. He opened his mouth in a silent squeal, and his gun fired into the floor.

Brody ran across the room and tackled Mike into the wall, knocking pictures to the floor. The gun fired again, this time into the ceiling. Brody grabbed the pistol with both hands and pointed it down the hall.

The Fixer appeared now, his gun at the ready.

Brody's hands covered Mike's hand, which still held his gun. Brody pulled the trigger, firing the weapon at the Fixer. A round hit the tall man in the shoulder, spinning him and throwing him to the ground.

The big man then yanked the gun back and forth out of Suicide Mike's hand, breaking his index finger with several sickening cracks. When he stood, he pointed the pistol down the hall at the Fixer, but the man was gone. The backdoor swung slowly closed.

From outside, Constable Emery Farnsworth hollered, "Freeze, police!"

Several gunshots were fired.

"I said freeze!" Farnsworth yelled in the distance.

Brody thought about pulling the trigger and shooting Suicide Mike, but Daphne watched him with eyes wide. Instead, he only pointed the gun at the biker.

He moved toward Daphne. "This is going to hurt," he said before yanking the duct tape from her mouth.

She howled in discomfort.

Brody then stepped back to Suicide Mike, who lay writhing on the floor in pain. Several times he tried to remove the knife from the biker's belt. Each time he reached for it, Mike moved and screamed in pain. The body of the white rhino lay next to him while its horn was still in the biker's skull.

He tucked his gun into his waistband and picked up the heavy knickknack. He then viciously clubbed Mike with the butt of the rhino. The man cried out, louder than before. Brody had to apply a second dose of pressure before the biker fell unconscious.

When Suicide Mike Eslick finally lay silent, Brody was able to remove the knife from his belt. He also pulled the keys to his motorcycle from the man's pocket. He then tossed the rhino to the floor and opened the knife. He began cutting the duct tape away from Daphne.

"What's going on, Brody? Who are these men?"

"I'll tell you later."

"I have a right to know!"

Brody stopped for a moment and met her gaze. Then he returned to cutting and pulling on the silver tape. "My name is Beau Smith. I'm not a naval officer, and I don't own a bookstore."

Daphne stared at him.

"Then what are you?"

"I'm a... well, I used to be a bookkeeper."

Chapter 38

Holding Daphne's hand, Brody stepped onto the front porch. In his free hand, he held the pistol.

A newer Ford pick-up screamed around the corner. Red and blue emergency lights were blinking in its grill. A siren wailed from somewhere under the hood.

"Here," Brody said, handing the gun to Daphne.

"I don't want *that*."

"You need to take it," he said. "I'm not allowed to have these anymore."

With a distasteful look on her face, she took the gun from him. "We are definitely *not* done with this conversation."

When the truck skidded to a stop, FBI Agent Max Ekleberry hopped out and put his cowboy hat on. While he trotted over, his head swiveled back and forth. "You okay, Beau?"

"I'm fine."

"Who's this?" Daphne asked.

"He's nobody."

"Nobody?" Ekleberry said. "Really?"

"Suicide Mike is inside the house."

"Eslick is here?"

"He's going to need a doctor. He's got a rhino horn stuck in his head."

Ekleberry looked at Daphne.

"It's true," she said. "A rhino horn."

"Anybody else in there?" the G-man asked.

"No, but there are a couple of prospects in the basement of the bookstore."

"What are they doing there?"

"Sleeping off a beating. I'm not sure how strong the latch is on the basement door. You might want someone to get over there and check on them."

Ekleberry glanced at Daphne, then returned his attention to Brody. "Your cover here is blown."

"That's an understatement," Brody said as he stepped off the porch with Daphne by his side.

Constable Emery Farnsworth walked up the street. His shoulders were slumped, and he shook his head.

"What's wrong, Constable?" Brody asked.

"He got away."

"But I heard gunshots. Didn't you shoot him?"

"He shot at me, but I didn't want to shoot him in the back as he was running."

Cops and their rules, Brody thought. But Farnsworth was taking it hard that he'd let the Fixer escape.

"It's okay," Brody said. "Everything will be fine."

"If I had my bike, I would have caught him."

Brody put his free hand on the officer's shoulder and gave him a small shake. "Emery, you did a great job. We saved Daphne."

He lifted his head and smiled. "We did, didn't we?"

Daphne smiled. "You're a hero, Emery."

The constable pulled his shoulders back. "We are, aren't we?"

"There's another FBI agent in the house arresting one of the guys. Why don't you go help him?"

Emery nodded several times. "Sounds good." He hurried up the sidewalk.

Daphne studied Brody. "*Another* FBI agent?"

"I told Emery that I was an FBI agent."

She frowned. "Do you ever tell the truth?"

Brody kissed her. "That's the truth," he said and kissed her once more.

When they finally broke, she didn't say anything. She just eyed him with suspicion but didn't let go of his hand.

A minivan turned the corner and raced up to them. Alice sat behind the wheel, and Carrie Fenton was in the passenger seat. When the driver's window rolled down, Brody could see the old waiter in the rear of the van.

"Alice!" Daphne said.

"Hey, kid. I see you met my friend."

Brody asked, "Find what you were looking for?"

"It took some time, but we did."

Daphne looked at Brody. Confusion played across her face.

Carrie Fenton sat in the passenger seat and stared straight ahead.

"She okay?" Brody asked.

"She's in shock. She'll be fine soon enough. She finally got to see what she writes about. It surprised her."

The big man eyed the waiter. "What about him?"

Alice smiled. "Him? We're going on a trip together. Someplace exotic."

"What about your cat?" Brody asked.

"Marlowe? What about him?"

"You should stop by the store and get him."

She shook her head. "No, thanks. That cat's a hazard. Besides, —"

"I know," Brody said. "Every bookstore needs a cat. Want me to tell Onderdonk you're okay?"

"Let him worry about me for a bit. When I come home from my trip, maybe I'll call him. I don't want to be found. After forty years, I need an opportunity to stretch my legs. You'll understand soon enough."

He did. Even though it had been less than a week, he already felt the weight of watchful eyes and governmental expectations.

Brody tapped the door. "You better get going then. I'm sure Ted's on his way."

Alice nodded. "Stay out of trouble. Be good, Daphne."

The minivan's tires chirped as it sped away.

Chapter 39

Brody and Daphne were outside the Italian restaurant, holding hands and examining the chopper.

"This was yours?" Her face scrunched in disbelief.

"Originally, it belonged to one of the club's founders, but I rebuilt her from the frame up." Brody's hand caressed the gas tank.

Sadness crossed Daphne's face. "You're leaving, aren't you?"

"The club knows I'm here. If I stay, evil men will keep coming to Pleasant Valley."

She looked away.

"There are two seats on this bike," Brody said.

"Do I look like a biker's girlfriend?"

"I'm not a biker anymore."

"What are you then? You're not a bookstore owner, and that's the guy I fell for."

"You can't fall for me if I'm on the run?"

"I don't want to be on the run," Daphne said. "I like it here."

He smelled the ocean's aroma and felt the humidity on his skin. He admitted to himself that he liked Pleasant Valley, too, but a lot of it had to do with the woman next to him.

A Chevrolet Impala pulled up to the curb. U.S. Marshal Ted Onderdonk sat behind the wheel. Brody knew he only had a moment to tell her how he felt before the lawman came up and destroyed the moment.

"Daphne, I—"

The door to the Italian restaurant opened, and the Fixer stepped out with a gun in his hand. "Get inside, rat. And bring the woman."

Brody instinctively pulled Daphne behind him. "You don't want to do this."

"It's already done," the Fixer said, leveling his gun at him. "I called the bosses. They know you killed Frankie the Dove. You think you had trouble before. Now the whole world is about to come down on you."

A car door opened behind Brody.

"You shouldn't have done that," he said.

The Fixer smirked. "Stop stalling. Get in—"

A gun fired, and Brody flinched. Daphne screamed and hugged him from behind. The glass door to the Italian restaurant splintered behind the Fixer.

The gunman looked around, trying to determine what had just occurred. Then he listed to the side, took a half-step to correct his balance, before shuffling forward several steps and dropping to a knee. He remained there for a moment as his chin fell to his chest. He blinked several times, each blink slower than the last. Finally, he stopped blinking altogether and tilted to the side. His head thunked on the sidewalk.

Onderdonk slowly approached, his gun between two hands. When he was near the Fixer, he kicked the man's weapon away. He reached down and pressed two fingers against the gunman's neck. When he was satisfied, he righted himself and put his firearm away.

"You didn't tell him to put his hands up," Brody said.

"That's for the movies."

"Don't think I owe you," Brody said, "because you created this mess."

"There's a whole pack of Satan's Dawgs coming up Interstate Ninety-Five. We need to get you out of here."

"I'll get myself out of town."

"Not a chance. You're my responsibility. I told you I would protect you, and I meant it."

"Not today," he said. He pulled the keys from his pocket and lifted his leg over the chopper. "I'll call you when I get someplace safe. I promise."

Daphne watched him with sad eyes.

"You coming?"

"I can't." She leaned in and kissed him on the lips. When she broke away, she stepped back and said, "This is my home. Besides, I've got to get back to the store." He watched her walk away. She never turned around to look at him.

For a moment, Brody thought about staying, but that would be suicide. The club was on the way, and the mob knew who had killed their underboss. Running was his only option—for him, Daphne, and Pleasant Valley.

"Hey," the marshal said. "That woman you had me look into, the one in Massabesic Lake? It wasn't Alice Walker."

"Don't worry, Ted. Alice will turn up. Trust me."

"What do you know?"

He put his hand on the motorcycle's key.

"Do not start that bike," Onderdonk said.

"I'll call you when I get somewhere safe. If you're here when the Dawgs arrive, tell them I went to Daytona Beach."

"Is that where you're going?"

The motorcycle revved to life.

"What about your cat?" the lawman asked.

Brody throttled the engine, piercing the quiet of Pleasant Valley.

"Do you want me to get him for you?" Onderdonk yelled over the roaring bike.

The big man gunned the engine twice and lifted the kickstand. The bike accelerated smoothly away from the curb.

He drove slowly down Main Street to the lighthouse and turned around, taking a final look at the ocean. Even though he knew now that Onderdonk had messed with the computer to send him to this quaint community, he wished it had worked out differently. Maybe this was where the universe had really wanted him to be.

But he wasn't a man to linger on wishes and dreams. He had to live in reality. And it was a fact the entire chapter of the Satan's Dawgs was on the way to Pleasant Valley. To save himself and the town, he had to leave now.

He revved the bike's engine before slowly driving through the center of town.

As he passed The Pleasant Peasant, he waved goodbye to Daphne. She watched him with tears in her eyes. He pulled his gaze away, swallowed with great difficulty, and continued up the street.

When he drove past Pleasant Valley Sundae, he scowled at a group of children eating ice cream. They giggled and jumped for no reason.

Several people looked into the windows of The Red Herring. Brody wondered if the marshals would continue to use the bookstore as a cover for the Witness Protection Program or if they would sell the business now.

Whether they did was not his concern, though. As he raced westbound on US 103, Brody Steele truly felt like a free man.

But while he drove away, a final thought occurred to him.

He hadn't finished reading *The Deep Blue Good-by* and would never get to talk with Daphne Winterbourne about it.

Beau Smith
returns in...

Cozy Up
to Murder

SPINACH CASSEROLE
(aka Joe's Special)

Courtesy of Gertrude von Finklestein

One pound ground beef
One small package of frozen chopped spinach (thaw
and squeeze out excess liquid)
One medium onion, chopped

Combine in a large frying pan and cook until meat
is done. Drain off grease.

Add:
One 4 oz. can of mushrooms, drained
One can Cream of Mushroom soup
½ cup sour cream
¾ teaspoon garlic powder
¼ teaspoon pepper

Combine all ingredients in the frying pan.
Spray coat an 8″ x 8″ pan and put the mixture in it.

Top with grated mozzarella or cheddar cheese.
Bake it at 325 degrees for 25 minutes.

A message from Gertrude:

*We modified this recipe from my father's favorite, Joe's
Special. It was originally from a restaurant in San Jose.
They cooked it in a frying pan and didn't use the soup or
sour cream. I changed it to a casserole.*

*For better flavor, use fresh chopped garlic and cook it
with the meat.*

ABOUT THE AUTHOR

Besides writing the Cozy Up Series, Colin Conway is the author of the 509 Crime Stories, a series of novels set in Eastern Washington with revolving lead characters. They are standalone tales and can be read in any order.

Colin is also the co-author of the Charlie-316 series. The first book in the series, *Charlie-316*, is a political/crime thriller and has been described as "riveting and compulsively readable," "the real deal," and "the ultimate ride-along."

He served in the U.S. Army and later was an officer of the Spokane Police Department. He has owned a laundromat, invested in a bar, and run a karate school. Besides writing crime fiction, he is a commercial real estate broker.

Colin lives with his beautiful girlfriend, three wonderful children, and a codependent Vizsla that rules their world.

Find out more at colinconway.com.